AGAINST THE WIND

By Scott Fields

Outer Banks Publishing Group
Raleigh/Outer Banks

Library of Congress Control Number: 2020930676

FIRST EDITION – February 2020
ISBN – 978-1-7341687-3-0
eISBN: 978-0-4635889-4-9

CHAPTER ONE

"Here I am, Lord," were his last words as his life slowly ebbed away. "I did the best I could," he said. His body relaxed on the bed. His mind was now fading with the memories of a long life that was lived with honor, dignity and a pure, nearly pious, devotion to God. This same God would now gather this mortal's soul into His arms and bring him home.

Shed no tears for this man for it was neither mortality nor humanity that controlled his life here on earth, rather it was the love of God that compelled him to serve his Master and his fellowman. He would succumb to no other, nor would he yield to mortal temptations, for a life devoted to the Almighty is promised sanctity and a hereafter life cradled Qin the arms of the Supreme Being.

"Here I am, Lord" were not only his last words but served as a guiding light for his very life. To, consciously, relinquish the temptations and promises of a mortal life to pursue a chaste and celibate, if not righteous life is an accomplishment that few mortal humans could achieve.

For this man was a priest and as such was prohibited from many of the humanly wants and desires that most others take for granted.

The old man's body twitched as tense muscles relaxed. Blood pooled in his organs as his heart slowed to only a few beats per minute. As his life slowly slipped away, a cascade of images marched across his mind's eyes. His last thoughts chased those images from his childhood love of fishing in the pond behind Grandpa's barn to the first time he drove a car and the first time he kissed a girl. Then, as his heart struggled to render one last beat, those memories faded and were lost forever.

CHAPTER TWO

The call came in the middle of the night, and even though I was expecting it, it still came as a shock. I could never figure why people couldn't have problems during the day. Bad things always seem to happen just after I get to sleep. I jumped in my car and raced across town to the hospital. Since I was no stranger to nearly everyone who worked there, a receptionist muttered a room number and went on about her business.

I never was a big fan of hospitals. Oh, I know they serve a useful purpose. Can't imagined what we'd do without them, but they sure give me the willies. Seems like they're always stickin' something in one of your openings. You can darn sure check your dignity at the door 'cause there ain't no room for it in a hospital.

I found his room on the fourth floor. Just like all of the other rooms, his door was wide open. There's one more example of dragging your dignity through the mud. Why they don't close doors and give people a little privacy is beyond me.

The room was dark except for one small lamp over his bed. It shone directly on him, but it was no bother. You see, Father Rinehart was in a coma, and there wasn't a thing in that room that was going to change that. Wasn't quite sure what happened, but I pretty much guessed it was a heart attack. Seen enough of them over the years to know this was a classic case.

I leaned over the side rails of his bed and stared at this man who had been my best friend for over forty years. Never really knew how old he was. Since I was sixty, that pretty much put him at around ninety years old. It was hard to think of him as being that old. He never slowed down, always on the go. He had way too many people who needed his help. Only thing was he never took time for himself. There were just too many people with some kind of need.

His snow-white hair seemed a bit messy, so I tried to smooth it out, but just like its owner, it was too stubborn to cooperate. The bright light illuminated all the age spots on his face, and I couldn't help but think I never really saw them before.

I know it sounds a bit weird, but I love that man. I guess I've loved him for most of my life, but never told him. I'm really not sure how he'd take it. Kinda scary, I guess, when a man tells another that he loves him, especially since I'm black and he's white. That might bother some folks, but I got a real good feelin' that God would approve.

I leaned over and took the liberty of fluffing his pillow. Wasn't much I could do other than that. Kinda looked as if he might be a bit uncomfortable, so I turned him so that he was flat on his back. Probably did no good seeing as how he was unconscious, but it made me feel better knowing I had done something for him. After moving him like that, I could now see his face. I stared at him for the longest time. For quite a while, I couldn't put my finger on it, but something seemed mighty strange. I stared into that face that I had known for all those years, and then it came to me. He was smiling. Father Rinehart was smiling. In all the years I knew him, I had never seen him smile. He took life way too seriously. Always worrying about this, that and the other. I'm surprised he didn't have a heart attack long before this one. Now that I think about it, I do remember him smiling at a joke I told him. Can't seem to remember what the joke was. I leaned back and thought for a moment.

"What was that joke I told you," I said aloud. "Had to have been a funny one to have cracked a smile on your face. Come on, Rinehart, what was that joke?"

From the back of the room, a soft voice broke the silence. "I know a few jokes," he said.

The unexpected voice startled me, and I jumped backwards. "Who's there?" I blurted into the darkness. I heard someone get to his feet and slowly walk into the muted light. I could just barely make out the figure of a tall, older man. He was wearing a black suit with a black hat. There was a small white spot at his neck that led me to believe he was of the clergy.

"Sorry to have frightened you," he said.

"I didn't see you there in the dark," I said. "I thought I was alone."

"I've been here for quite some time," he said. "I should have made my presence known before this, but I was afraid that I would startle you."

"Well, it worked."

"Sir?"

"You managed to startle me."

He was a big man with large shoulders and a slim waist. His face was rugged, and yet he had a warm smile. With his overall stature and handsome appearance, he looked dignified and quite possibly commanded respect from all who knew him. He thrust his hand in my direction. "My name is Livingston. I'm the bishop in this area."

"Bishop Livingston," I said taking his hand. "I have received many memos from you."

He gave me quite a puzzled look. After all, I was dressed in jeans and a tee shirt. "And you are?" he asked.

"Father O'Brian," I said.

Darned if his face didn't get an even more puzzled look.

"I know what you're thinking," I said. "What's a black man doing with a name like O'Brian? Actually, that's a long story. Were you the first to arrive here?"

"Actually, the nurse told me that there were two men and a woman here before me. She said that it seemed so bazaar that Father Rinehart was wearing a poker face before they arrived and had this strange smile after they left."

"Isn't that a bit peculiar?" asked Tony, as if thinking out loud.

Livingston glanced down at Rinehart. "Have you known Father Rinehart for very long?"

"Seems as if I've known him all my life," I said.

The Bishop removed his hat and took a deep breath. "Unfortunately, I'm here to give him the last rites, that is if the doctor feels it's necessary. The sad part is I hardly know the man. Oh, we've talked on the phone and the like, but I really never got to know him. Heard a lot of good things about him. Lord knows, I've tried to get him to retire, but he wouldn't hear of it. Said there was still too much to do to complete his mission for God, whatever that meant."

"That's our Eddie," I muttered.

The bishop nearly jumped. "Eddie? Who is this Eddie?"

"Rinehart here," I said with a slight trace of a smile. "Bet you didn't know his first name is Edward."

"Yes, I knew his name was Edward," he said almost pompously. "You must know that we rarely refer to a member of the clergy by his first name and certainly never by a slang name."

Why I used that name I'll never know. I should have known that would bristle the hairs on his neck. "Sorry," I muttered but with my smile still intact.

"You're bordering disrespect for the man," he said with a growing indignation.

My smile grew wider. "Bishop Livingston, nobody has more respect for this man than I do."

"Then why would you call him Eddie?"

"It was a long-standing joke between us," I said. "In the beginning, it made him madder than you are right now, but over the years, it became a private joke between us. Actually, if there was any one man who needed a laugh from time to time, it was this one."

There was a pause. I was quite sure the man was trying to change the subject.

"Was this his first heart attack?" he asked.

"Far as I know," I said.

"Well, we can always hope he pulls through."

"Yeah, and maybe it will finally slow the old turd down."

I could see out the corner of my eye his hands as they landed on his hips. I cringed as I waited for another ass whoopin'.

"Father O' Brian, you are not only disrespectful but a bit flippant as well."

Now I knew at the time that I should be a bit more patient and understanding since he really had no idea what kind of relationship we had, and, yet, that's what was making me mad. It seemed to me that he was passing judgment before getting the facts.

"Bishop Livingston, we seem to be getting nowhere. Is there something I can do for you?"

"Well, I was hoping someone could give me a little background about the man, but I'm not sure you're the one to do it."

Now he was really starting to get to me, but I knew I had to mind my mouth, 'cause after all, he was my boss. "Well, that's your choice," I said. Having said that, I walked to the back of the room and sat down.

"Are you leaving?" he asked.

"Why should I?"

"Well, I'm here to administer the last rites. There's no need for the two of us."

"You can do what you want, but I'm not leaving."

"Why not?"

"He was and is my very best friend," I said. "If there is any hope at all of his recovery even if it is only for a minute, I'll be here."

"Very well," he said and settled into a chair beside mine. He crossed his legs and cleared his throat. The next thing I knew he was bobbing his leg up and down. I do believe he was as uncomfortable as I was considering the words that were exchanged. "All things considered, I suppose I've been a bit verbose." He paused. "I apologize."

"Don't mention it," I said with a bit of a smile. "Like I said before, there's no way you could have known about Eddie and me. Whoa, let me make a change here. There's no way you could have known about Father Rinehart and me."

The Bishop paused then smiled. "In other words, keep your opinions to yourself until you hear the whole story."

There was no way I was going to answer that one, so I dodged it the best I could. "Would you like to hear about Father Rinehart?"

The Bishop stood, took off his coat and hung it on the back of his chair. "Why not. I have ample time."

I settled back in my chair and turned to the ceiling. There was so much to tell, and I wasn't quite sure where to start.

"To be honest with you, our story really begins a long time ago in a place called Cass Corridor on the south side of Detroit. Now I'm sure you've been exposed to ghettos in your life at one time or the other, but you've never seen anything like Cass Corridor. Even the name sounds dreadful. It's so bad that the Detroit Police don't even go down there. It's about like the old Wild West with the sheriff out of town. I've never seen anything like it. Why, they even drive right through stoplights like they weren't even there. I'm a bit surprised they don't have more accidents than they do. There are all kinds down there. Back then, there were mostly drug dealers, and I suppose nothing much has changed in that regard.

Now I know you're wondering what this has to do with Father Rinehart. I will get to him real soon, but first you need to meet a young black man by the name of Tony Franko. I know what you're thinking. What's a black kid doing with a name like Tony Franko? Well, his mother married an Italian guy. They had Tony, and six years later, they had his brother Odell. Where they came up with a name like Odell is beyond me. It could be Italian, but it sure doesn't sound like it.

Tony's father left home when Tony was a teenager, and they never heard from him again. Things got real bad, and what little money his mother had saved was soon gone. They were facing eviction if they didn't come up with some money real soon, and there were no honest jobs to be had in the Cass Corridor.

It was early March. Spring was just around the corner, as they say, but you couldn't tell it by the weather. Old Man Winter hadn't given up yet and was dumping huge amounts of snow. It was just getting dark, which was the time all businesses in the area closed. From five o'clock in the winter months to nine in the summer, whenever the dark of night was approaching, that was closing time for Cass Corridor. Only a fool stayed open past dark.

Tony had been watching a small party store owned by a man by the name of Pierce Brooks. Tony made mental notes of his closing procedures and the time he locked the doors.

It was nearly two o'clock when Tony and his brother stopped in front of the store. He could see Mr. Brooks as he went about his business of closing the store. Odell stared through the window at the man then turned to Tony.

"What are we doing here?" he asked.

Tony turned to his brother. "We're going to rob this place," he said with a shaky voice.

"What?" asked Odell with a look of horror.

"We're going to rob this party store."

"You can't be serious."

"If we don't come up with some money, we're going to get kicked out of the house. Mama needs our help."

"Well, this is no way to get money."

"You got any better ideas?"

Odell ran his hands through his hair. "Maybe we could get a job or something."

"There are no jobs. Besides, the landlord is coming tomorrow for the rent money."

Odell turned and stared at the party store. Mr. Brooks had already turned off lights in the back of the store. "What makes you think we can do this?"

"I've been checking out this place for the last two weeks. He follows the same routine every night, and I've never seen him with a gun."

"So this is where you've been going every night after dinner."

"It should be a piece of cake," said Tony. He then pulled a small handgun from his coat pocket and slid it into Odell's hand.

"What's this?" asked Odell staring at the weapon in his open hand.

"What do you think it is?"

"I'm not going to shoot anybody."

"I know you won't, 'cause that gun doesn't have any bullets."

"No bullets!"

"I couldn't afford them," said Tony. "Besides, Mr. Brooks won't give us any trouble."

Odell paused, his mind racing over the facts. He grabbed Tony's arm. "Please, Tony, don't do this. Something bad is going to happen."

"I'm telling you we'll be fine," said Tony. He then pulled two ski masks from his pocket. "We'll wear these, and he'll never know it was us."

"I'm begging you not to do this, Tony. I have this feeling about this. Someone is going to get hurt."

Tony hands him a mask. "Everything will be alright. We'll be in and out of there in no time."

Tears welled up in Odell's eyes as he slid the mask over his head. He gripped the gun in his hand as he followed Tony into the store.

Unfortunately for Tony and his brother, Mr. Brooks had rehearsed over and over what he would do in the event of a holdup. The fact was he had already been robbed so many times, he had prepared himself for any future robberies and vowed that someone was going to die.

It all happened so fast. It was almost like one of those cop shows you see on TV. Tony and Odell never had a chance. It was as if Brooks knew all along that they were coming. As soon as he saw them walk in with masks and guns, he ducked down below the counter. Tony froze. He had never expected that. It was a long counter, and Tony had no idea where the man was and what he was doing. Tony panicked. He fell to his knees and started to crawl towards the counter when suddenly from the other end, Brooks popped up. He was pointing a gun in their direction. Odell jumped and swung his gun towards Brooks. In an act of self-defense, Brooks fired at Odell striking him in the chest. Odell collapsed onto the floor, his gun falling out of his hand and sliding across the floor.

Tony turned to see his brother lying on the floor with blood oozing from his chest. He jerked the ski mask from his head and crawled to his brother. Tony gently took off Odell's mask and cradled his head in his lap.

"It hurts, Tony," he said. "It hurts bad. Make it stop hurting."

Tony began to sob. "I'm so sorry, Odell. I didn't mean this to happen."

Brooks picked up the phone and called the police.

"It wasn't your fault," said Odell.

"Oh, yes, it was."

"I shouldn't have turned my gun on Mr. Brooks," he said, his voice weakening.

"I shouldn't have brought you with me. You didn't want to do it in the first place."

Odell closed his eyes. "Yeah," he said softly.

Tears flowed down Tony's cheeks. "You said that someone was going to get hurt."

Odell's eyes were still closed. His voice was but a whisper. "I don't want to die," he muttered. "I don't want to..."

You know, it seems like all my life I've set parameters, the biggest this and the smallest that. What was the best movie of all times and the worst? Seems like all of those things that were the best and the worst meant very little and were always changing, but the loss of a child will always remain as the worst tragedy in life. Poor old Tony just sat there on the floor holding his brother's lifeless body for what seemed like hours. In fact, when the police arrived, they had to pry his fingers from Odell. It all happened in a split second of time, and yet would stay with Tony for the rest of his life.

Tony's trial didn't make any headlines. In fact, it only lasted a few hours, and Tony was off to prison. Seemed like Tony just didn't care anymore. His mother got kicked out of her house, and his brother was dead, and it was all his fault. At least, that's what had somehow got implanted in his brain. Life didn't seem worth livin' anymore. Tony just went through the motions. He only spoke when he had to, and then it was usually to answer someone's question. Even when they dropped him off at prison, he showed no emotion and said not a word.

Tony Franko was transferred to a medium security facility in Marion, Ohio. It was an unimposing building in the middle of a vacant field north of town. In spite of its low-risk inhabitants, it still had high fences with coiled barbed wire and guard towers on all sides. There had been escapes from Marion Correctional Institute, but all would eventually be returned. With few exceptions, most of the escapees were inmates who had gained respect from prison officials and were classified as trustees. With such a title, they were allowed to work on the prison farm gaining them access to sunshine and the outdoors. Every once in a while, one would get brave or he might have a problem with his girlfriend and would simply walk off the grounds. Some of the more daring escapes involved cutting fences and crawling over barbed wire. These were far less successful but made great reading material in the morning newspapers.

Tony was locked up with a white man by the name of Lloyd Cobb. Lloyd was a likeable kind of guy, but he never knew when to shut up, and quite frankly wasn't the brightest bulb in the bunch. He had successfully robbed a jewelry store and only a week later tried to sell one of the stolen necklaces just a block from the store. The man he approached just happened to be the owner of the jewelry store.

A uniformed guard opened the cell door and Tony walked in. He took a seat on a wooden chair in the far corner of the room.

Lloyd walked across the room and stuck his hand in Tony's face. "Hi, I'm Lloyd Cobb, your cellmate. Who are you?"

Tony simply held his hand for a moment then pulled it away. "The name is Tony," he muttered.

"Tony," said Lloyd. "That's a nice name... for an Italian. Never heard of a Negro called Tony."

"Negro?"

"Well, whatever you guys call yourselves," said Lloyd. "By the way, why are you in here?"

"Attempted robbery."

"Weren't no attempted in my sentence. I up and robbed a jewelry store. Got caught a week later selling the stuff back to the owner."

Tony slowly turned to Lloyd. "You sold the stolen goods back to the owner?"

"Well, I didn't know he was the owner," said Lloyd. "I'm not that stupid."

Tony studied his new home. It was small with dark gray walls with no windows. The only accommodations were a desk, two chairs, bunk beds and a toilet. He wasn't expecting much, and that was a good thing.

"What's it like in here?" asked Tony.

"It's okay," said Lloyd. "Mind your own business, follow the rules and you'll be out of here in no time."

"What rules are those?"

Lloyd leaned back as if he was about to tell a long story. "You know how in prison movies, there is always a bad guy who is the boss. Sometimes there are two bosses who vie for the top dog position, which usually cause wars between the two parties. Marion Correctional Institute has just one boss and there's no doubt in anyone's mind that he is the boss. His name is Luigi Rossi, and either you are on his side or you are against him."

Tony forced a smile. "So he's a tough guy, huh?"

"He is the law here in our little world of captivity. He makes the laws, and he enforces them."

Tony sneered. "Sorry, but I'm not impressed."

Lloyd seemed to bristle a bit, almost like Tony had insulted him. "You might have been a big shot on the outside, but in here you're just another stiff doing time. And if you know what's good for you, you'll stay out of his way."

"Hey, I'm from Detroit," said Tony. "Where the weak are eaten."

Lloyd gave Tony a look that pretty much said that he had spoken his last on the subject of Mr. Rossi. "You keep on with that kind of thinking, and you'll go out of here in a bag. Like I said before, keep your nose clean, and you'll do fine."

Tony leaned back against the concrete wall and folded his arms across his chest. Lloyd couldn't help but notice that the look on Tony's face said volumes. It was obvious there was more than just being locked up that was bothering Tony. He had the look of a troubled young man.

"You got family?" blurted Lloyd.

"Huh?"

"Family. Do you have any family?"

Tony paused. "Yeah, I got a mother."

"Only child?"

"Huh?"

"Are you an only child?" asked Lloyd.

"What the hell difference does that make?"

"Statistics show that kids born with no brothers or sisters usually are quiet and shy sometimes even socially retarded."

"Did you just call me a retard?"

Lloyd got this wide-eyed look and started to back pedal. "No, I called you shy and quiet."

"Damn, son, you just called me a retard, and we just met," said Tony with a scowl. Then he said something to completely change the direction of their relationship. "You gotta know me a lot longer than that to realize I'm a retard."

Lloyd paused for a moment. I think he wanted to see a sign of a smile from Tony. After all, he had already insulted him once.

One of Tony's strong points was his infectious smile, and it was about that time that he let one go. Lloyd laughed hysterically. I think more from relief than anything else.

Tony seemed to change that day. Up until that time, the death of his brother weighed heavily on his mind. He couldn't stop thinking about it. Of course, he blamed himself. Hell, who wouldn't? Odell didn't want any part of it, and, yet, Tony forced him into it. You'd have to be pretty cold-blooded not to feel guilty to some degree or other. For some reason on that day, Tony let it go. Maybe he came to realize there was no sense beating himself up about it or maybe his mind just went into some defensive mode and discarded the event completely from his brain. For me, I knew that boy couldn't stay depressed for too long. You see, Tony was the kind who firmly believed in one motto, and that was growing old is mandatory, growing up is optional. Whether he knew it or not, Tony lived by that motto. He lived to be an old man, but he never did grow up.

It was nearly a week later before Tony met up with Mr. Rossi. I guess it would be fair to say that Mr. Rossi met up with him. Tony and Lloyd were eating lunch in what most folks would call the cafeteria. It was actually known to those who had to eat there as the choke-and-puke. They were eating their meals, talking quietly among themselves when Luigi set a tray of food beside Tony.

"Mind if I join you?" asked Luigi.

Tony stopped eating and turned to Luigi. He was a big man, grossly overweight with no hair and a twitch in his left eye that never seemed to quit.

"It's a free world," said Tony. "Well, kinda."

Luigi sat down and seemingly from no where two huge goons sat down as well.

"You don't mind if my two friends join us, do you?" asked Luigi.

"Is this some kind of welcoming committee?" asked Tony.

Luigi laughed halfheartedly. "Yeah, I guess you could call us the welcome wagon, huh, boys?"

Tony turned to the two men. They hadn't quite discovered the humor of the moment, and, in fact, were still staring at Tony with menacing scowls.

"Your friends seem a bit upset," said Tony.

"Oh, don't mind them," said Luigi with a smile. "They're not easily amused."

"That's not a surprise," muttered Tony.

"Let me introduce myself, my name is Luigi Rossi."

"Tony Franko."

"Tony Franko, you say. Unusual name for a Negro. Are you Italian?"

"Pop was."

"That makes you part Italian," said Luigi. "We're practically relatives." He laughed so loud that his belly shook and tears ran down his face. Tony smiled but didn't say anything. I think he realized that it was in his best interest to behave.

"You're not from Detroit, are you?" asked Tony.

"No. Why?"

"I had heard of a Rossi. He was some kind of mobster or something."

"I lived in Detroit for a spell," said Luigi. "Wasn't what you would call a mobster. In fact, I was in the trash hauling game. Great town, that Detroit."

"Why do you say that?" asked Tony. "Most people hate living there."

"Lotta dumb people live there. Real easy to screw them out of their money."

Tony's smile disappeared. "You mean a lot of blacks live there, don't you?"

"I didn't say that."

"You didn't have to, but that's what you meant."

Rossi grew angry. "Hey, kid, don't start with me. I got nothing against your kind. I like to take money from whites just as much."

Tony paused, and I'm sure he told himself to calm down. He decided to change the direction of the conversation. "So, do you pretty much run things in here?"

"I'm just a resident here just trying to get along."

"Then, what do you want from me?"

"Nothing. Not a thing," he said with a look of shock. "We just wanted to welcome you and to let you know that if there is anything you need just let me know. I like to take care of all my friends."

Tony ate a bite of food. "But we're not friends."

"How can you say that?"

"We just met," said Tony. "We're just acquaintances."

Rossi got up from the table. His goons did the same. "That's where we differ, my friend," said Rossi. "I consider everybody my friend until they give me reason not to. Don't you think my way is a much more Christian thing to do?"

"I suppose you're right, Mr. Rossi," said Tony.

"It's Luigi to you. Like I said, you're a friend, and my friends call me Luigi."

"Okay, Luigi," said Tony. "Thanks for stopping by."

Tony resumed eating. All the time, Lloyd had remained quiet and had in fact seemed frozen.

After they walked away, Lloyd returned to life. "Do you know who that was?" asked Lloyd.

"Yeah, that was my old buddy, Luigi."

"Luigi Rossi isn't friends with anybody. He's just setting you up."

"Setting me up for what?"

"He's going to call on you as a friend to do him a favor."

"What kind of favor?"

"Who knows, but it won't be to pass out hymnals in the prison church. He's going to ask you to do something illegal. That's for sure."

"You're just jealous."

"Jealous of what?"

"Jealous of my friendship with Luigi."

Lloyd gave a half-hearted laugh and spit on the floor. "I ain't a gonna argue the point with you any more, but you just mark my words. You're gonna hear from your old buddy, Luigi, and you ain't gonna like what you hear."

Tony seemed to dismiss the whole incident and finished eating his meal.

Lloyd and Tony never did become all that good of friends. To me they seemed to be the perfect misfits ever put together. And I don't think it was a racial thing, even though Lloyd did admit that his folks were a bit prejudice. Let's face it, they were two different guys from two different worlds. Lloyd was proud of the fact that he was a farmer, and Tony was from the streets of Detroit. The only real thing they had in common was the air they were breathing. Not that they didn't get along. Good Lord, I don't think they ever had an argument. Of course, they weren't together that awful long. As you'll soon find out, Tony didn't care for the accommodations and soon moved out.

About a month later, it was early spring and the planting season for the farmers in the area and for the prison system. Planting massive gardens and fields of corn was not just a way to keep the prisoners busy. It was a very important means of feeding the inmates of not only Marion's population but the surrounding prisons as well. The gardens of tomatoes, beans and potatoes were harvested in the fall, canned and distributed to the other prisons. The corn was used to feed the cattle at the Mansfield Reformatory where they slaughtered the animals for meat. The prisons were virtually independent and self-supporting. I supposed it was designed that way. Sure kept the costs down to the taxpayers.

Now I'm not sure how it happened, but the next thing you knew Tony found himself classified as a trustee and was allowed to work outside on the farm. He was about as surprised as anyone, figured that because of his age and the nature of his crime, they must have been willing to take a chance on him. So, just weeks after entering the Ohio penal system, Tony Franko was a trustee. I'm pretty sure that set some new record of some kind. Whether it did or not, the bottom line was Tony was outside of the prison working in a garden with no fence around him. Oh, make no mistake, there were guards watching over Tony and the other trustees. In fact, they were carefully placed so they wouldn't miss a thing. Tony didn't seriously consider escaping, but he didn't rule it out either.

It was about this same time that Tony was trying to get along in his new environment. He had purposely avoided confrontation and even conversation with other inmates with the idea that the old adage that said something to the effect of be seen and not heard would serve him well and quite possibly keep him out of trouble.

Unfortunately, that was not to be. You see, Luigi Rossi was not the only boss in that prison. There was another man by the name of Carlos Mancini who was equally powerful, controlled a large portion of the inmates, and was feared by many. Now Tony didn't directly cross Carlos. In fact, it was purely an accident when Tony rounded a corner and ran right into a man called Bruno who just happened to be one of Carlos' lieutenants. Bruno was a big man, strong as an ox but not all that skilled in the art of fist fighting. Generally, his ominous appearance frightened most adversaries away, most all of them except for Tony Franko.

After the brief and seemingly innocent collision of the two men, there was small talk, and as they continued on their separate ways, Bruno uttered an ethnic slur that caught Tony's ear. It's funny when you look back on life and recognize the crossroads you faced along the way. At the time, they didn't seem like they were all that important, but later you wonder how life would of turned out if you'd only taken the other road. This was one of those crossroads in Tony's life, and looking back there's no doubt that he took the right path.

"What did you call me?" asked Tony.

Bruno stopped and turned. "You heard me the first time."

"Why would you call me a name like that?"

"Because you are one."

Tony could feel a fire starting inside and stepped closer. "I'm surprised the vocabulary of a big dumb ass like you includes such a word."

Bruno walked over and stood in front of Tony. He was so close he was nearly touching him. I think it was a move to intimidate Tony because he towered over him by nearly a foot.

"You calling me dumb?" asked Bruno in a voice that was even deeper than before.

Tony smiled as he glared up at the man. "You couldn't pour piss out of a boot even if you had instructions."

Bruno kicked one foot back for better balance. "You little..." he muttered and swung a fist at Tony at what we used to call a haymaker.

Fortunately for Tony, he was quick and agile and was able to duck under the attack. I don't think Bruno quite understood how street-smart Tony was and how many times he had been forced to defend himself. Tony knew no fear. He had been fighting since he was old enough to walk. It wasn't that Tony was that hard to get along with, it was just the way life was on the back streets of Detroit.

Tony jumped back and brandished his fists to warn his attacker.

"Let it go, mister, 'cause you're gonna get hurt."

I don't think Bruno was ever very skilled at fighting because he simply took another swing at Tony. This time, Tony blocked his fist with his arm and swiftly kicked the big man in the groin. For a brief few moments, Bruno froze, then like a house of cards he dropped to the floor. He moaned and groaned clutching his crotch and rolling around on the floor. Such a fighting technique has never been considered to be acceptable or fair, but it has always been considered to be effective.

It was later that same day that Tony met up with his roommate, Lloyd. Tony was sitting on the edge of his bed when Lloyd pulled up a chair. He was just as about as excited as a kid on Christmas Eve.

"Is it true?" asked Lloyd with an excited look.

"Is what true?"

"Did you actually kick Bruno Mullins in the nuts?"

"His name is Bruno? Even his parents knew from the get go he was going to be a big dumb ass."

"Oh, my God!" said Lloyd. "You don't have any idea who Bruno is, do you?"

"Yeah, he's someone who shouldn't call me names."

"Bruno Mullins just happens to be the right hand man of Carlos Mancini," said Lloyd. "That's all."

"Who is Carlos whatever?"

"Who is Carlos Mancini? Man, where have you been? He's the godfather in here. He's the head man, the head dude."

"I thought Rossi was the head of the garden club around here," said Tony running his hands through his hair.

"We have two bosses in here, and they don't get along very well."

"Good grief," said Tony. "Doesn't anybody teach their kids how to play with others?"

Lloyd looked around and lowered his voice as if someone might be listening. "Well, I have good news and bad news."

"Give it to me," said Tony.

"The bad news is Carlos wants you dead."

"What's the good news?"

"Luigi wants to meet with you."

Tony paused. "A godfather wants to meet with me. That can't be good."

"It's better than what Carlos wants."

"Good point," said Tony. "Guess I'll see what he wants."

It was two days later before Tony met with Mr. Rossi. Arrangements had to be made to insure Tony and Mr. Rossi's safety, and prison guards needed to be bribed to allow the meeting to take place.

It was early afternoon when Tony approached a guard standing in a hallway. Tony stopped in front of the man, and he opened a door to a broom closet. Tony cautiously walked inside. Mr. Rossi was standing under a bare light bulb hanging from the ceiling. The light from the bulb cast shadows on his face that made him look like some kind of a monster.

"We meet again, Tony Franko," he said sticking out his hand.

"I am honored to see you again, Mr. Rossi," said Tony cautiously taking his hand.

"Don't forget, it's Luigi to you."

Tony paused as he shook his hand. "Okay...Luigi."

"You're a brave man, Tony," said Luigi. "Assaulting that big lug like you did. That took a lot of nerve."

"He and I didn't hit it off so good," said Tony.

"I hear he called you something you didn't appreciate."

"Never did like that word."

"Well, unfortunately, you seem to have upset Mr. Mancini in the process."

Tony forced a smile. "That's what I hear. I suppose I'm in a bit of a fix."

Luigi put his arm around Tony. "Son, we need to get you out of here, because that man will eventually see you dead. I understand you work on the farm as a trustee."

"Yes, sir."

"Tomorrow at two o'clock, something will happen to create a diversion. I want you as close to the road as you can get. A car will stop for only three seconds. You must be there. They will not wait. Do you understand?"

"Yes, I understand."

"We will have a change of clothes for you and take you somewhere that the officials will not find you."

Tony paused for a moment. He needed to ask the man a question but didn't want to upset him. "I appreciate what you're doing, but I really need to know why. Why are you doing this for me?"

Luigi patted Tony on the back. "You did me a great service when you hit Bruno Mullins. He nearly killed one of my men, and I've been trying to get at him ever since. You did me a favor, and one favor deserves another."

"Technically, I didn't do it as a favor to you."

Luigi smiled. "Doesn't matter. The results are the same regardless of the intentions."

Tony smiled and shook his hand. "Thank you sir. I won't forget this."

"Just remember you only have three seconds to get in that car."

"I will."

As you recall, Luigi mentioned something about a diversion. Good Lord was that ever an understatement. It was late in the afternoon when it happened. All of the farm equipment was contained in a huge building that set in an open field near the gardens. Without warning, an explosion lit up the sky. It ripped that building to splinters and sent a mushroom cloud miles in the air. I don't know where they got their explosives, but it wouldn't have surprised me if it was some kind of a nuclear device. Needless to say, all of the guards left their posts and ran to the site. It was a vision to behold. Tony was so captivated he almost forgot why it had happened.

The next thing he knew, there was a black limousine stopped just ten feet from him. He dropped his tools and ran across the field. A door swung open, he slid inside and the car sped away. Tony turned and glanced out the window. Nobody had even noticed that he was getting away.

Tony settled back into his seat and turned to the two men sitting beside him. They were big men, Tony could tell. They had heads that were as big as half of Tony's body. They were dressed in black suits wearing black hats and had a look on their faces like somebody had just died. Now I know that Tony was grateful for getting out of there, but he wasn't all that sure what he was getting into.

Tony smiled at the men. "I hope you all know how much I appreciate what you're doing for me, but I was wondering if you could tell me where we're going?"

No reaction. The two men said nothing. In fact, they just stared at the road ahead, until one of them sat up in his seat and pointed at the road ahead.

"Pull over there next to that clump of trees," he said.

For a moment there, Tony thought it was all over. There he was in the middle of a country road with nobody around for miles, and they were stopping the car. From where Tony was sitting, it sure didn't look good. Then one of the men shoved a paper bag at Tony.

"Go over there behind that tree and change clothes," he said.

Tony had mixed reactions. He was relieved that he wasn't being executed for some reason, yet he wasn't sure why he was changing clothes and what he was changing into.

"May I ask…"

One of the men cut him off. "Just go change."

Sensing a bit of impatience in the man's voice, Tony opened the door and got out. He walked behind a tree and opened the bag. "Good Lord," muttered Tony as he pulled out a priest outfit. "They can't be serious." He put on the clothes and returned to the car. One of the men actually snickered as he slid across the seat.

"Ain't nobody in the world gonna believe I'm a priest," said Tony.

"That ain't my problem," said one of the men. "We're going to dump you out in some small town. If I were you, I'd find the nearest Catholic Church and start kissing ass."

"Some plan," said Tony sarcastically.

"We can turn around and take you back to the prison."

"That's alright," said Tony. "I'll take my chances."

CHAPTER THREE

Father Livingston got out of his chair, stretched and leaned over Rinehart's bed. "You're right about one thing."

"What's that?" I asked.

"Father Rinehart does have a peculiar smile on his face."

I got out of my chair and joined him. "I hope we get a chance to ask him what's so funny."

Father Livingston turned to me with a strange almost confident look on his face. "We will," he said.

"I don't understand, Father," I said.

"It is a certainty that he will come out of this coma, of that I am sure of."

"Believe me, I'd like to think you're right, but I've seen too many of these conditions, and I will be surprised if it happens."

Then Father Livingston did something I'll never forget. He put his arm around my shoulders and looked me in the eyes. He had a look of confidence that made me think he had inside information. "You will get your chance to ask Father Rinehart about his smile."

I turned back to Rinehart and thought about what Father Livingston had just said. I wanted to believe him. I wanted so much to at least say good bye to Rinehart. No, scratch that. I would never give up. I would never say good bye. That would never do. What I really want to say to this dear man is how much I love him.

There was something about this man called Father Livingston that left me uneasy, and yet he gave me a warm feeling, a feeling of trust and a feeling that everything is going to be all right. I really can't say why I felt uneasy. I guess I had never met a man quite like him. It seemed like he knew more than he let on.

"Pardon me for saying so, Father Livingston, but I somehow get the feeling that you either know Father Rinehart or knew him a long time ago," I said.

"Can't say as I have," he muttered.

"You being his boss, I would have thought it was inevitable that you would have met him."

"I conduct my business from an office. Don't get out in the field all that much."

"That surprises me as well."

"What's that?"

"Not getting out in the field," I said. "You look like the type who would dislike a desk."

Livingston forced a weak smile. "Too much to do, and most of it can be handled by phone."

"Yes, I guess that figures," I said, still not satisfied with his answers.

As if to change the conversation, Livingston said, "Enough about us, tell me what happened to Tony. They were driving him to a small town."

"Well, it was nearly dark when the car pulled into town. I don't think Tony had ever seen a town that had only three stoplights. Hell, even when you included the surrounding farms, there were less than nine hundred residents. He dropped him off on a side street, gave him some free advice and sped away. The free advice was a suggestion that he find some way to get involved with the church. Everyone in that part of the state is going to be looking for an escaped convict, and his only chance would be to blend in. Since the town of LaRue, Ohio had never had a black resident, his chanced of blending were slim.

It was nearly dark and the air was getting colder. From where he was standing, Tony could see the downtown area and started walking in that direction. It was smaller than he had imagined, with the business district only three blocks long. He walked past the grocery store, the hardware store, one of the gas stations, and Bailey's Farm Implements. He was soon in the residential section and standing in front of the Catholic Church. It was a small structure in need of paint but not unexpected for such a small town.

A sign was posted near the front wooden doors. Tony moved closer to read it. It was something about a pancake breakfast to raise money for a place called LaRue. Obviously, Tony had never heard of LaRue, but it did strike a spark and give him a great idea. He glanced at the bottom of the sign. It was signed by Father Rinehart.

To the left of the church was a two-story colonial house nearly as big as the church. It was richly designed in Victorian style with ornate features including a tall, oak double door entrance. Tony knocked on the door. A neatly dressed, older woman appeared.

By this time, the night air had turned cold, and Tony blew into his hands as he pranced up and down.

"Is Rinehart here?" he asked.

With one hand the woman grabbed the side of her head in horror. "I beg your pardon."

"Is the padre home…the pastor…whatever you call him?"

"Are you asking if Father Rinehart is available?"

"Isn't that what I just said?"

"Wait here," she said and closed the door. A few minutes passed before the door reopened. "He's much too busy to see anybody tonight. Please try again tomorrow." With that she closed the door.

Tony knocked on the door again but got no response. He stepped off the porch and walked around to the side of the house. A light shone from one of the windows, so Tony walked over and peered inside. An old, white-haired man dressed in black was bent over a desk. Tony couldn't help but notice that whatever he was doing, he was intently involved to the extent that he looked a bit stressed.

Tony knocked on the window. No reaction. He rapped a little louder. This time the old man looked up and leaned over to see out of the window. Tony smiled and pointed at his collar. Rinehart stormed out of the room, and Tony ran to the front porch. The front door opened just enough for Rinehart to stick his head out.

"Yes?" blurted Rinehart.

Tony stuck out his hand. "I'm Tony Franko. I was sent here by the head fish-eater."

Rinehart paused as he gathered his wits. "The head fish-eater?"

"Yeah, you know…the boss…the guy you report to."

"Do you mean the bishop?"

"Yeah, that guy."

"Just today, I talked with the bishop on the phone, and he said nothing about you or your arrival, so go away," said Rinehart and closed the door.

Tony tapped on the massive door again. Rinehart stuck out his head again. "Are you hard of hearing?"

"I don't think so," said Tony. "Why?"

"Because I told you to go, and you're still here."

Tony held his hands in the air. "You can't leave me out here in the cold."

"Watch me," said Rinehart and slammed the door shut.

Tony tapped on the door again. This time Rinehart swung the door wide and stepped onto the porch.

"What is it, son?" he said. "Is there some reason you hate me? Did I marry off your girlfriend to some other guy?"

"I told you that I was sent here to help you raise money for that Hill thingy."

Rinehart paused. "You mean LaRue?"

"Whatever."

"Well, who are you?"

"I told you, I'm Tony Franko."

"I caught your name. What's your title? Are you a priest?"

"I'm a priest-in-training kind of thing."

"Never heard of such a thing."

"It's new."

"They didn't have such a program when I was in training."

"They most likely didn't have electricity back then either."

Rinehart's eyes lit up. "Listen here, young man..."

Tony opened the door wider and stepped inside. "You know, we can discuss all this tomorrow. Right now, I could use a bite to eat and a bed, because my ass is draggin'."

"You are a verbose young man," said Rinehart.

"I got a feeling that ain't good."

"Where's your luggage?"

"Ain't got any. By the way, the head dude said for you to buy me a change of underwear. I've worn these for four days straight, and you ain't gonna believe what they look like."

"So you want me to feed you, buy you new clothes, and provide a place for you to sleep," said Rinehart. "Is that about right?"

"Nothing gets by you."

Rinehart grabbed Tony's arm and started for the door. "I don't know who you are, but you are not staying in my house."

Tony braced himself against the wall and turned around. "You know your boss really wanted me to help with this LaRue thing. I think he's going to be disappointed when he learns you went and threw me out of your house. Besides, he wanted you to train me on how to be a monk."

"A monk?"

"Yeah, a monk."

"What in the world would I know about being a monk?"

"Aren't you a monk?"

"I'm a Catholic priest for goodness sakes, not a monk."

"Well, I'll be," said Tony. "Here I thought they were one in the same. Well, what's it going to be? Are you going to let me stay here for the night, or are you going to upset your boss?"

Rinehart paused. "Okay, Mister…"

"Franko…Tony Franko."

"Okay, Mr. Franko, you can stay for the night, but I'll be calling the bishop in the morning."

"That bishop fella gave me a message to pass on to you," said Tony.

"And what might that be?"

"He said for you not to bother him on this matter."

"I don't believe you," said Rinehart, slightly angered.

"He said you're like an old woman sometimes and should just suck it up."

"Suck it up?"

"You know…roll with the punches."

Rinehart said nothing. He just stared at Tony.

"He said you can either take me in, or he's busting you down to the church janitor."

"Your room is at the top of the stairs, and lasagna is being served in the dining room."

Tony smiled. "Let's eat."

"Lord, I wish you could have seen that boy run to the dining room. Wasn't hard to imagine that lasagna was the favorite dish of a boy named Tony Franko. He had just started his third helping when in from the kitchen came a woman by the name of Wanda Jackson. She was a middle-aged, greatly overweight black woman who was the housekeeper, driver and cook for Father Rinehart. She had been with him for nearly twenty years, and in spite of her irascible nature and disagreeable disposition, she wouldn't leave him even if he stopped paying her. In spite of their common ethnic backgrounds, Wanda didn't care much for Tony. In fact, it's a wonder she let him stay there.

She walked across the room and poured fresh coffee in a cup for Rinehart.

"Wanda Jackson, this is Tony Franko. He was sent here to help me with a few matters."

Tony paused and wiped his mouth. "Glad to meet you, Wanda," said Tony with a smile.

"It's Mrs. Jackson to you," she said with a sneer. "Besides, I ain't never seen no black Father before, especially one as young as you. Where you from, boy?"

"Detroit."

"I don't know what you're up to, but you ain't no more a priest than I am."

"Mrs. Jackson, I'm surprised at you," said Rinehart. "Mr. Franko was sent here by the Bishop. He deserves our respect."

"Oh, he'll get the respect he deserves, alright."

Tony held out his hands. "Wanda, I'm just a trainee. I'm here to learn from the head boss over here."

"You call me Wanda again, and I'll bang yer head with a fryin' pan."

"Mrs. Jackson, I'm surprised at you," said Rinehart.

She turned back to Tony. "Name me three books from the Bible."

"Huh?"

"You heard me. Anybody wantin' to be a priest has surely read the Bible. Name me three books."

Tony paused. "Martin, Luther, and King."

"See what I told ya, he's a wolf in sheep's clothing," she said, then pointed a finger at him. "I got my eyes on you, boy."

Tony got up and walked over to her. "Mrs. Jackson, what do I have to do to convince you that I mean no harm?"

"Move away. Go back to Detroit or where ever you came from. If the truth be known, I'll bet you just got out of jail."

"Mrs. Jackson, I've never known you to be so rude to a guest in this house," said Rinehart."

"He's not a guest in this house, he's an intruder," she said with a raised voice. "You mark my words, he's up to no good. I've seen a million boys just like him beggin' and stealin' on the streets of Detroit, and he ain't no different from the rest."

There was a silence that fell on the room, a very uncomfortable and awkward silence. Finally, Tony stretched and yawned.

"It's been a long day," he said. "Mind if I go to bed?"

Rinehart was still a bit in shock from Wanda's reaction to Tony's arrival and even more ashamed of how they both treated him. "Like I said, your room is at the top of the stairs."

"What time is breakfast?" asked Tony.

"Be dressed and downstairs by seven o'clock," said Rinehart.

"You mean seven in the evening?"

"Seven in the morning," said Rinehart. "I like to get to the diner right after it opens."

"Seven in the morning!" said Tony. "I'm not what you would call a morning person. Maybe I can get Ms. Jackson here to fix me some breakfast somewhere around noon."

"Lord, I'm gonna kill that boy," muttered Wanda.

"Mrs. Jackson doesn't start work until nine," said Rinehart.

"Well, if we're up and at 'em at seven, why can't she be a workin'?"

"She likes to sleep in," said Rinehart with a trace of a smile.

"Sho' don't seem fair."

Wanda turned and started for the kitchen. "Ain't much fair in Wanda's world."

Rinehart smiled. "See you at seven."

***

By seven the next morning, the sun was just coming up. Rinehart slid on his coat and stared up the stairway. He could hear Tony fumbling around, so he was sure that he was awake. Just then, Tony appeared. He had on the same clothes that he had worn the night before, his eyes were swollen until they were nearly closed, and he was weaving back and forth down the stairs. He got to the end of the stairs and stared at Rinehart.

"So this is what the world looks like in the middle of the night," said Tony.

"It's not the middle of the night," said Rinehart. "It's seven in the morning."

"It might be seven to you, but it's the middle of the night for me."

Rinehart sighed. "Do you have a coat?"

"No."

"It's twenty-two degrees out there," said Rinehart. "Here take one of mine."

"Thanks," said Tony taking a coat from Rinehart.

"Why do I get the idea you're going to be nothing but problems for me?" said Rinehart.

"A pain in your butt?"

"That too."

Rinehart opened the door and hobbled out with his cane.

"War injury?" asked Tony.

"What?"

"Did you get shot in the war or something? Pretty hard not to notice that you're using a cane and limping."

"Did you ever consider the fact that some things are none of your business?" asked Rinehart.

"Where are we going?" asked Tony.

"To the diner."

"Aren't we driving down there?"

"I don't drive."

"Well, how do you get around?"

"Mrs. Jackson drives me when I need to go out of town, otherwise, I walk."

"Do you mean we're walking all the way downtown?"

"It's only two blocks, for crying out loud," said Rinehart. "I can see the diner from here."

"Well, for one thing, it's cold out here, and, for another, I hate walking."

"Do you ever stop whining?"

"Just long enough to gripe and bitch," said Tony.

"You sure do plenty of all three."

"Is this the whole downtown?"

"Yeah. Why?"

"It's just a little bit bigger than a breadbox."

Rinehart stopped and turned to Tony. "Maybe we should put bars on all the windows to make you feel at home."

"Whoa, there partner," said Tony. "That shot you fired sailed right over my bow."

The Village Kitchen was a small diner with tables and chairs that had wobbled back and forth since Truman was in office. There were two windows that had the same dead flies on the sills since even before Truman. The wooden floor creaked so loud when someone was walking that the other patrons had to stop talking until they were gone. I guess cleanliness is not all that important when you're the only place in town to eat. You can either stay at home and cook your own meal, or come on down and join your neighbors and the dead flies.

In spite of all that, they did serve very tasty food and large portions at that. Breakfast was their specialty, and everyone in town was particularly fond of the breakfast special. In fact, those who didn't order it were either from out of town or considered to be a little bit strange. It was the usual fare of eggs and bacon, toast, meat, and hash browns, but what made it the favorite of every resident in town was the fact that it was served on a platter. I swear there was enough food on one of those platters to feed a family of four. You see, in the small village of LaRue, it wasn't always the taste that made a dish popular. Getting the most bang for your buck was held in the highest esteem. The cook's name was Buford Hickman. Most days, Buford served edible food, and some mornings when he was in a good mood, it tasted pretty good. But on the mornings he had a hangover, you never knew if your food would be ice cold or burnt. Raymond Ridgeway was always the first through the door every morning, and he carried a bottle of aspirin just in case Buford had been hitting the bottle the night before. Raymond would check on Buford, and if he was sitting on a stool and holding his head, he would shake out a couple pills for him. They didn't always kick in right away, so sometimes it wasn't until the lunch crowd showed up that the food got any better.

One of the unique features of the diner was a long table that ran right down the middle of the eating area. I'm sure it wasn't just one table. In fact, it was about four normal size tables end to end and covered with a variety of tablecloths. It was right there at that table that all of the farmers met every morning. Lord almighty, you never heard such a ruckus. Every morning it was the same thing. There was name-callin', dirty jokes, lies and gossip. Most of the men showed up every morning just so the others wouldn't be talkin' about him. Everyone pretty much had his own place at the table. Once in a while, someone would sit in a different spot usually to whisper some juicy gossip to the man in the next seat, but just as soon as its rightful owner would show up, he would immediately move to his place at the table.

Now like I said before, Wanda didn't start work until nine, so Rinehart had been eating his breakfast at the diner for years. He had his place right at the head of the table. And don't think they gave Father Rinehart special treatment just because he was a man of the cloth. Sometimes, they seemed to be even harder on him. After all, he grew up with these men and even went to school with most of them.

Mind you now, this small farming community had never been blessed with anything other than white, flag-waving, God-fearing residents. The only black people they had ever seen was on the cover of National Geographic, and here was Father Rinehart with a young black man wearing priest garb. Oh, sure, we had Wanda, but for some reason she did't count. Somewhere in the white man's rules, it surely must state that a black woman working for a white man is permissible 'cause nobody has ever complained about it. Must be it reminded them of slave labor or some such thing. Besides, there ain't nobody I know who would want to tangle with Wanda Jackson.

As soon as he opened the front door, as always, all eyes turned to him. This time, all chitchat and small talk came to a halt. They stared. Some with open mouths as the two men went straight for the head of the table. Rinehart took his seat, and Tony pulled an empty chair over next to him.

Rinehart rubbed his hands together. "Good morning, gentlemen."

From the other end of the table, a lone voice muttered, "Morning, Eddie."

Tony turned and smiled. "Eddie?"

"Never mind," whispered Rinehart.

"Is your name Eddie?"

"It's Father Rinehart to you."

"But your first name is Eddie?"

"It's Edward...Father Edward Rinehart. Some of these bozos like to call me by that name."

"You can't even force yourself to say that name, can you?"

"Give it a rest, will you?"

"So, Eddie," said Charlie Sprague, fighting laughter, "Who's your friend?"

"This is Tony Franko," said Rinehart. "He's here to help me with a few things." The room was dead quiet. "You may have noticed that he is not white."

"No shit," said one of the men.

"He's down here from Detroit learning to be a priest," said Rinehart.

"And you're the one teaching him?" said Earl Bass. "The kid ain't got a chance in hell of learning anything."

A low murmur of laughter spread down the table.

"By the way, Eddie," said Fred Munson. "Emma Thompson's cat is stuck in the tree again."

"So, why are you telling me?"

"Well, you got it down the last time."

"That doesn't make it my job."

"I thought you priest guys were suppose to do things like that, saving animals and whatnot."

"Why don't you get it down, Fred?"

"Afraid of heights," said Fred. "Besides, I hate cats, and I'm not all that crazy about Emma."

It was about that time that the waitress, Clara Butts, showed up carrying six plates of food spread across one outstretched arm. She dropped them one at a time in front of the men.

"Hey, I only got one sausage patty," said Willard Barrow.

"You need to drop a few tons," said Clara. She turned to Rinehart. "Eddie, the same? And what about your friend?"

Rinehart turned to Tony. "He'll have the same."

"Oh, so, I can't order for myself? Black boy from Detroit too stupid to read a menu?"

"You got enough problems, besides the menu is only for looks," said Rinehart. "They only serve the special."

"What if you wanted pancakes or a waffle?"

"Guess you'd better stay home and fire up your own skillet."

Small talk, mumbling, and hushed laughter began to spread around the table. After all, this was quite a day for the small farming community. Never before had a black man set foot in the town, and here was one sticking both feet under the same table as the likes of Travis Heller, the mayor of LaRue.

"So, Eddie," said Cletus Trumble. "Is your new friend here going to live with you over at the parsonage?"

"He isn't my friend, and yes he's living at the parsonage for now."

"With Wanda already living there, that kinda makes you a minority," said Cletus with a smug look on his face.

The room broke out in laughter.

"How can you say he ain't your friend?" said Willard. "You both dress alike, and you're practically hooked at the hips. You look like a pair of salt and pepper shakers."

Again the room was filled with laughter.

"That sounded racist to me," whispered Tony.

"You're surrounded by rednecks," said Rinehart. "What did you expect?"

It was about that time that Clara showed up with breakfast and coffee for Rinehart and Tony. She gathered up empty plates and cups and started for the kitchen.

"Clara, you're mysteriously quiet this morning," said Rinehart. "Anything wrong?"

The place grew silent just to hear her answer.

"Mavis called in," she said. "Something about her aunt fallin' and breakin' her hip. If I had time, I'd feel sorry for her, but I'm busier than a two-peckered billy goat."

Tony glanced at Rinehart. "Two-peckered…man, you people sure talk funny."

Rinehart turned to Tony and whispered in his ear. "How the people in this town accept you depends on how you act and what you say right here and now. Within thirty minutes of our leaving this restaurant, everybody in this town will hear the report on you made by these retards sitting at this table. So, try to make a favorable impression."

Tony paused. The room went silent. It was if they all were expecting him to say something meant to impress everyone.

"I once knew a black man who became a farmer," said Tony. "Of course, they said he was too dumb to do anything else."

Rinehart covered his face with his open hand. "Good Lord, help us."

"Young man," said Fred Munson. "You say you're from Detroit. What's it like up there? What does a kid like you do for fun?"

Tony smiled. "Drugs, a little burglary, and lots of murder."

The room froze.

"Just joshin' ya. We're too young for drugs. We do that other stuff though."

Nobody moved.

"Just kiddin' you guys. We played in the streets, tried to make a buck by mowing lawns or run errands for old people. Basically, we survived."

Earl bristled and sat straight in his chair. Everyone knew that if anyone would ask a sensitive question it would be Earl Bass. Nobody was quite sure if he was truly interested in knowing the answer or that he simply liked to stir the stick as they say. From the years that I knew Earl, my guess is he liked to ask questions that made people squirm in their seats. He'd go to a hanging just to see the guy twist in the wind.

"Tell me something," said Earl with that smug look he often got on his face. "How do you feel about race relations?"

"Dear God," groaned Rinehart.

"Who asked that?" asked Tony.

"I did," said Earl holding up a hand.

"What's your name?" asked Tony.

"Earl Bass."

"Earl, I'm glad you asked that question," said Tony with a smile. "I'm a NASCAR fan myself. Anybody else have a question?"

Everyone laughed except for Earl. He stood this time, the smile gone from his face. "I mean how do you feel about white people and black people livin' together?"

Rinehart leaned over and whispered, "Be careful."

"You know, Earl," said Tony. "Your ancestors were about as dumb as a box of rocks."

"Huh?"

"Paying good money for a bunch of lazy Africans was one dumb move. Think about it, Earl. It doesn't matter if they are free help, if they don't do anything, they ain't worth a whole lot. But the real villains in this story was not your ancestors, not by a long shot. The real villain was the African guy selling his kin and friends to the white guys just to make a buck. How can you get any lower than that?"

There was much head nodding and mumbling at the table.

"Actually, if you white folks were smart, you'd pack us all up and send us back to Africa," said Tony. "After all, we Africans don't appreciate what we got right here in America, and let's face it, you white people ain't got no need for us anymore. The free help thing went away when you fought that God-awful Civil War."

Rinehart glanced at the faces of the men sitting around the table. They were all smiling and talking softly to each other.

He turned to Tony and whispered, "That's the most racist thing I ever heard."

"Made 'em happy, didn't it?"

Rinehart looked at the men once more. "God help us all."

Tony took a bite of his food. "Still proud of your goober friends?"

Before Rinehart could answer, Earl stood again. "That was a crowd pleaser of a speech, young man, but now I have another question for you."

"Fire away," said Tony.

"Do you believe in God?"

"Mr. Bass, I believe in God with all my heart," said Tony. "Do you?"

"Since you're new here in town, you wouldn't know this, but it's a pretty well known fact that I'm an atheist, always have been, always will."

Tony sipped his coffee." Pretty proud of it, huh?"

Rinehart whispered, "Leave it alone."

"Not only proud of it, but willing, ready and able to debate the issue with anybody, anytime, anyplace," said Earl. "You seem a bit cocky, young man, are you interested in defending your God in a healthy debate?"

"Who will you be defending?" asked Tony.

"Nobody," said Earl. "Just think of me as the prosecutor and you the defender."

"And God is on trial?"

"I think you've got the idea."

"Hold on there, Earl," said Rinehart. "I haven't seen you this excited since Cletus over there let you watch his sheep while he was on vacation. Now, leave the boy alone. This is no way to treat a stranger."

Tony leaned over to Rinehart. "What's this? You came to my defense?"

"Don't push it," said Rinehart.

"I knew I'd grow on you."

"I defended the collar around your neck," said Rinehart. "As far as you're concerned, I wish you'd go back to where ever you came from."

Now most people would take that kinda personal and, in fact, might be offended, but not Tony. In spite of his background and upbringing, Tony was always the optimist. He had a positive outlook on life and never took no for an answer.

"I don't get it," said Tony. "You get a good-looking kid like me who is free help, and you complain."

"I don't want any help from you or anybody else. I've been getting along all these years without it, and I'm doing just fine."

"I think the bishop knows something you don't," said Tony with a coy smile.

"And what's that?"

"You're getting on in years."

Rinehart turned towards Tony, his voice getting stronger. "Listen here, you little shit. I can still outwork you any day of the week, and I could kick your ass as well."

"Father Rinehart, I'm surprised at you. Should you be saying potty words like that?"

"My God, you're infuriating," said Rinehart. "I could just…"

"So tell me again," said Willard pointing a finger at Tony. "Why the hell did they send that boy here to this hick town?"

"He was sent here to help out at LaRue," said Rinehart.

The whole place froze for a moment. Even Clara, who was pouring coffee refills, stopped in mid-stream.

"You're going to send that boy out there to work with Larry Joseph?" asked Willard. "You can't be serious."

Now that last statement made by Willard caught Tony's attention. And then when he noticed all of the shocked looks, he knew something was wrong.

He turned to Rinehart. "Okay, who is this Larry Joseph?"

"He's the man who is building LaRue," said Rinehart.

"Why are all these people in shock? You'd think I was going to work for Hitler himself."

"Larry Joseph can sometimes be a bit difficult to get along with."

"You mean he don't like colored-folk."

"Huh?"

"What you're trying to tell me is that he's a racist."

"Good Lord, you couldn't be further from the truth," said Rinehart. "Larry Joseph truly loves all people."

"Well, then, what's the problem with him?"

"He's not unlike me in the sense he works alone. There have been others offer help to no avail."

"What is he some kind of weirdo?"

"That's been said, but either way, you're wasting your time."

Then Tony got this big cocky smile on his face. "Well, he hasn't met up with Tony Franko."

"Hey, Eddie," shouted Cletus. "The hardware store has one last football helmet for sale. You might want to think about getting your friend one before he goes out there to meet Larry."

Rinehart turned to Tony with a scowl. "I told you I didn't need your help, and now I get this. Why me? Why did you have to come into my life?"

"I guess God was just looking after you," said Tony with a smile.

"And that's another thing," said Rinehart. "You told Earl that you believe in God. Was that the truth?"

"Not a bit of it," said Tony. "Don't believe in that hocus pocus."

"You don't believe in God?"

"Never did."

"Then why are you in training to become a priest?"

"Are you kidding?" asked Tony. "It's probably the best job in the world."

Rinehart scowled. "And how do you figure that?"

"Think about it, you get paid a good wage for working a couple hours on Sundays, and ya got the rest of the week to do nothing."

Rinehart paused as he tried to control his temper. "You are probably the most infuriating…"

Tony took a bite of his food. "You wanna jaw about this later? My breakfast is getting cold."

Now I've known Eddie for a lot of years, and I never saw him quite like he was when Tony first came to town. I truly am surprised he didn't kill him or at least plaster his mouth shut. Seemed like no matter what, Tony was saying and doing the wrong thing. Rinehart tried to ignore him in the beginning, but he soon learned that Tony wasn't the kind of guy to be ignored. In fact, he was just annoying enough that most everyone avoided him. The walk back from the diner certainly didn't win Tony any points.

Tony was short of breath trying to keep up with Rinehart. "How do ya do it?" asked Tony.

"How do I do what?" asked Rinehart his pace even quickening.

"The walk back-and-forth everyday. How do you do it?"

"It's only a few blocks."

"A few blocks? It's got to be two miles if it's an inch."

"Mr. Franko, I don't think I've ever met someone who complains as much as you do."

"And that's another thing," said Tony nearly out of breath. "Shouldn't I be called Father Franko or some such thingy as that?"

Rinehart stopped and turned to Tony. "You are the most arrogant and disrespectful young man…"

"Well, what about it?"

"What about what?"

"What about that Father thing? I like the idea of some old white guy calling me father."

Rinehart froze. He stared blankly into Tony's eyes. He then turned and started walking again this time with a purpose. "I must call the bishop about you. I still don't think he really sent you here."

"I'm warning you," said Tony. "You're going to make him mad."

"I'll take my chances," said Rinehart. "I don't know what you're up to, but my guess is the bishop has never heard of you."

Rinehart marched up the steps to the front door of the parsonage. He let himself in and slammed the door in Tony's face.

"It's about time you boys got home," said Wanda on her way to the kitchen.

"Why?" asked Rinehart. "What's wrong?"

"Belva Bowdry called. She's having another one of her spells."

"Let me guess," said Rinehart. "She needs her medication."

"Hey, you're the one who started the drugs on wheels," she said walking towards the kitchen.

Tony laughed. "What is she talking about?"

"Never mind," said Rinehart starting for the door. "We've got errands to do, and you're driving."

Tony fell into behind. "Why me? Why am I driving?"

"You need to start doing something around here."

"You don't know how to drive, do you?"

"Why do you always have to be so confrontational?" asked Rinehart.

"What does that mean?"

It was about that time that Rinehart opened the garage door, and Tony saw for the first time a 1949 F-100 Ford truck. In fact, Tony froze as he stared at the bright red vehicle that had obviously been green at some time in the past as revealed by the stone chips near the wheel well.

"You don't expect me to drive that piece of junk, do you?" asked Tony.

"Piece of...How dare you call this fine machine a piece of junk."

"You have to admit that it's seen better days."

"This is a 1949 F-100 Ford truck, one of the finest vehicles ever made by man. It will be around long after you're gone."

Tony smiled. "I doubt that," he muttered.

"What did you say?"

"Nothing."

Rinehart scowled. "Don't you ever think about driving this vehicle unless I'm with you."

"Oh, sure, boss," said Tony with a smile.

"Don't oh, sure, boss me. You're not allowed to drive this truck without me. Now get in, and let's see how you do."

The two men got in the truck. Tony stepped on the clutch and turned the key. The engine roared to life. It purred softly until Tony gunned the engine. Rinehart shot him a look but said nothing. Tony smiled. He slipped the gearshift into first, revved the engine and popped the clutch. The truck lurched forward jerking Rinehart back in his seat.

"Slow down," said Rinehart.

"What?"

"Slow this truck down, right now."

"We're not even doing 25 miles per hour."

"That's 10 miles per hour over the limit."

"No, it isn't," said Tony, pointing out the window. "See there. The speed limit is 25."

"The speed limit here in town is 25. My speed limit is 15, so you're ten over."

"Good Lord, what's that all about?"

"It's really quite simple," said Rinehart. "You never drive this machine without me or over 15 miles per hour."

"That's ridiculous," said Tony. "It must take you forever to get where you're going."

"This is a classic vehicle and needs to be treated with respect."

"You treat this truck better than you do me," muttered Tony.

"The truck serves a function," said Rinehart glancing out the window. "So far, all you've been is a pain in my ass."

"And that's another thing," said Tony. "When are you going to fix it, so that people call me that Father thingy?"

"That's not going to happen."

"Why?"

"You have to be ordained, and you'll never make it."

"How can you say that? You don't know what I'm capable of doing."

"I know that you're undisciplined, ill-mannered and incapable of learning anything as complex as the priesthood."

"I'll bet if I was white, you wouldn't be saying that."

Rinehart slowly turned to Tony. His eyes glowed through tiny slits. "Mr. Franko, if you ever say that to me again, I'll throw you out into the street, and this masquerade or whatever you're up to will be finished. Do you understand?"

Tony was wide-eyed with shock. "Yeah. Sure."

"What did you say?" asked Rinehart.

"I said yes, sir."

Rinehart pointed out the window. "Now turn down that street."

"Who is this Belva gal anyhow?" asked Tony.

"I meant to warn you about her. She is a very cantankerous old woman who was the cook down at the diner for over forty years. Belva took orders from people for all those years, and she isn't taking anymore."

"You sure have a lot of cranky, old people in this town," said Tony.

Rinehart pointed again. "There she is."

Tony turned to see an old woman in a flowered dress hobbling down the sidewalk towards the curb. She had a scowl on her face, and in spite of her bad hip that caused her to limp, her pace was fast enough that few could keep up.

"Is she riding in the back?" asked Tony.

"No, she's not riding back there."

"Well, where is she going to sit?"

"Right up here between us."

"You've got to be crazy," said Tony. "From looking at that old woman, I can tell that someone is going to die today."

Tony brought the truck to a stop, and Rinehart got out to let her in. Now there's an old saying that says something about if looks could kill. If that were true, Rinehart would have lost his driver right there on the spot. Belva didn't say anything. She just stood there staring at Tony. Finally, she climbed up and slid across the seat. There was a dead silence as Rinehart got back in the truck and closed the door. Belva continued to stare at the young man. Every second seemed like an hour.

"Who the hell are you?" she finally asked.

"I'm Tony Franko."

"What the hell is a Negro doing in LaRue?"

Rinehart leaned forward. "Now, Belva."

She then turned to Rinehart. "And where the hell have you been? You're fifteen minutes late."

"Well, we had to…"

"Where the hell is Wanda? I don't like this young man."

"Why don't you like me?" asked Tony. "Is it the color of my skin?"

"Quite frankly," said Belva. "I ain't never been around a Negro before. I ain't real sure if I like Negroes or not."

"Then why do you say that you don't like me?"

"Do I need a reason?"

"That's not good enough," said Tony. "I want to know how you can instantly say that you don't like me."

Rinehart cleared his throat. "Alright, you two. Settle down. This is just a trip to the drug store. You don't have to be the best of friends for that."

Now Tony was not really happy with Rinehart's solution but dropped the banter just the same. After all, it was just a trip to the drug store. He might never see Belva Bowdry again.

Tony stopped the truck in front of a faded and paint-chipped Rexall sign. Rinehart slid out of the truck and held the door open for Belva.

"Now you wait here," she said as she slid across the seat. "Don't go driving off and leaving me here."

"Don't tempt me," muttered Tony.

Rinehart climbed back into the truck and closed the door.

"What a nasty woman," said Tony.

"She is not a nasty woman," said Rinehart. "She just gets a little cranky at times."

"Why do you have to drive her down here?"

"Someone has to."

"So you're elected because you're the local do-gooder?"

"Things are different here in a small town. I wouldn't expect you to understand."

"I understand one thing, and that is your Belva Bowdry is a bigot."

"No, she isn't," said Rinehart.

"Yes, she is. She flat out told me she didn't like me."

"Belva Bowdry shows no discrimination. She hates everyone, white or black."

"Don't cover for her. I know when a white person hates blacks."

Rinehart paused and turned to Tony. "I know you're young and inexperienced, and for that reason I'll forgive you for that last statement, but you've just proved that you're no better than a member of the KKK."

Tony bristled. "Man, you'd better explain yourself."

"Some simple-minded redneck labels you by the color of your skin, and you label Belva Bowdry by her one statement."

"So you're trying to tell me she doesn't hate blacks?'

"Belva Bowdry has been supporting a young black boy somewhere in California for years. Somehow she found out about this boy losing his parents in a car accident, and the next thing you know she is sending checks to support him. I don't know how she does it. Her only support is a monthly retirement check that probably isn't enough to keep a bird alive. All I'm asking is that the next time you want to pull out that race card, just take the time to be sure you're right. Trust me. It would be real easy to dislike you because of who you are rather than because of your race."

After Rinehart's little speech, Tony was pretty much in shock. Nobody had ever explained things quite that way. He had always figured that if a white person hated a black, it was because of the color of his skin. He was about to respond when Belva pounded on the door. Rinehart slid out and let her in.

"Okay, take me home," barked the old woman.

Tony paused then smiled. "Sure thing, Mrs. Bowdry," he said.

Tony turned the truck around and started down the road. He was driving nearly 20 miles per hour, but Rinehart didn't say a word. In fact, it was completely silent in the truck. Now that I think back, I would guess the silence was a way of saying I'm sorry.

Tony stopped at an intersection. He glanced one way and then the next. It was about that time that he spotted something that would start a chain of events that would change his life forever. A truck was stopped in the middle of the street blocking the path of a horse-drawn buggy. Two men stood in the street facing one another. From his long beard and distinctive black hat, one was an Amish man while the other was a young, rather large burly man dressed in jeans and a plaid shirt. Tony slowly turned the corner and parked next to the curb.

"What are you doing?" asked Rinehart.

"Isn't that one of those Amish guys?" asked Tony.

"Yeah. Why?"

"I thought I read that Amish people don't believe in fighting."

"So?"

"I don't know, but it looks as if that big dofuss is picking a fight with that Amish guy."

"So what's that got to do with you?" asked Rinehart.

"I'm gonna stop him."

"No, you're not."

"What do you mean by that?"

"Just what I said. Stay out of it."

"Aren't you a man of God?"

"Yes."

"Does a man of God watch while someone beats on another defenseless man?"

Rinehart pointed at a truck parked on the other side of the street. "See that man sitting in that truck?"

Tony squinted. "Do you mean the guy with the stupid cowboy hat?"

"That guy with the stupid cowboy hat is Frank Bower. He owns most of this town, and he's nobody to mess with."

"What's he got to do with what's going on here?"

"That goon talking to the Amish man is Buddy Butler. He works for Frank, and Frank hates Amish people."

"So, since Frank hates Amish people, that gives him the right to terrorize this family?"

"You have no idea what you're getting into," said Rinehart.

Tony turned to see Buddy push the Amish man until he nearly fell. Now, all of the instincts that Tony had learned from the streets of Detroit rose inside the young man. He had seen such brutality all his life, and he wasn't about to sit by while an innocent man was being abused. Tony opened the door and slid out.

"Don't do it, Tony," said Rinehart.

"You want me to sit back while a man abuses another man?'

"It's none of our business," said Rinehart.

Tony leaned against the open window of the truck, his face next to Rinehart's. "Do you think Jesus would have said it's none of our business?"

Rinehart said nothing.

Tony marched down the street. He stuck out his hand and helped the Amish man get to his feet then helped brush him off.

"Who the hell are you?" asked Buddy his voice dripping with sarcasm.

"I'm Tony Franko," he said thrusting out his hand. "And you must be Buddy Butler."

Buddy ignored the outstretched hand. "I don't know who you think you are in that priest outfit, but you're about to get your butt kicked."

Tony smiled as he returned his hand to his side. He stepped closer, bending back his head to talk to the man who towered over him. "Buddy, you seem to be a reasonable man. Think about this situation from my perspective. Oh, I'm sorry. You probably don't understand that word, so let me rephrase that. Think about the fact that you are hurting this man from my point-of-view. I am a man of God as even you can see from the clothes I wear. I was also raised on the streets of Detroit. Do you have any idea what that means, Buddy?"

"Get to the point, butthead."

"The point is I can hurt you really bad or just make a body part ache for a day. That's the point," said Tony.

"By this time, Frank Bower was getting impatient. Not only was he worried that the local marshal would show up but citizens of the town getting involved.

"Buddy," shouted Frank. "Get on with it."

Buddy quickly turned to acknowledge Frank then fell into a fighting stance. "You know what?" asked Buddy. "You gonna get the ass-whoopin' that I was gonna give that guy over there."

Buddy took a powerful swing, and Tony easily ducked under it. Mind you, this was back somewhere in the sixties, and not many people had heard of karate or martial arts. Tony not only had heard of it, he was an expert at it. There wasn't much that Tony learned while growing up, but a cousin had been kind enough to teach him at an early age how to defend himself. I am fairly certain that if Tony had been formally tested, he would have been considered a black belt.

After Buddy's unsuccessful jab, he was left completely vulnerable, and Tony knew it. He could have easily crippled Buddy or even struck a blow that could have been fatal. Instead, Tony thrust his foot into Buddy's knee. As Buddy buckled and fell to the ground, Tony kicked him square in the groin. It's always been my opinion that no man really wants to do something like that to another man, but sometimes it's necessary. One thing is for sure, it certainly gets their attention if not serving as an equalizer.

It happened so fast that poor old Buddy didn't know what happened. The next thing he knew he was on the ground and in real pain.

Tony leaned over to help him to his feet when he heard a loud, booming voice from behind him.

"What's your name, boy?" asked Frank

Tony spun around to find the larger-than-life Frank Bower standing in front of him. Tony was caught off guard for a moment but soon gave Frank one of his famous smiles. "My name is Tony Franko. What's your name...boy?"

"Whoa," said Frank forcing a smile. "I can see we're a little sensitive."

"Why would you say that about me? You're the one who has yet to give me your name."

Tony must have hit a nerve because the smile disappeared from Frank's face. He leaned over and jerked Buddy to his feet. "Tell me something," said Frank. "Why did you have to go and hurt my friend here?"

"Ask your friend," said Tony. "He started it."

"Now let's cut the crap, Mr. Franko," said Frank pointing at Tony. "Stay out of my business. Do you hear me?"

"Well, if pushing around an innocent man is your business, then we have a problem."

Frank started for his truck with Buddy close behind. "The Amish are my business, so stay away from them."

Tony watched as they walked away. He turned to the Amish man and stuck out his hand. "Hi. My name is Tony Franko."

"I'm Riley Hoagland," said the man taking his hand.

"Are you okay?" asked Tony.

"I'm fine. I want to thank you for helping me."

"Not a problem."

"Are you new to these parts, Mr. Franko?"

"Yes, I am. Why?"

"It's just that I've never seen a priest who is…"

"Black? Is that what you were going to say?"

"Well, actually, I was going to say I've never seen a priest as young as you."

Tony smiled, a sheepish smile but a smile all the same. "I'm not really a priest yet. I'm still in training."

"Ah, yes. Well, once again, thank you for your help."

Tony shifted his weight as if to change the direction of the conversation. "I know it's known of my business, but why is Frank Bower pushing you around?"

"Mr. Bower doesn't like or should I say has never liked my people," said Riley. "Up until a few days ago, it was just another person who didn't approve of us, but that's all changed."

"What has he done?"

"There's a creek that flows through his land and continues past our farms. We depend on the water from that creek to nourish our animals. Mr. Bower has blocked the flow of the creek until it has now dried up. If he doesn't allow the water to flow again, our animals will die."

"Can he do something like that? It sounds illegal."

"It's on his land," said Riley. "Besides, there is no one in town who is going to stand up to Frank Bower."

Tony turned to see the truck and Rinehart and Belva waiting inside. "I have to be going."

"Once again, I thank you, Mr. Franko. You are truly a man of God."

Tony paused with a look of shock. "Nobody has ever said that about me," he muttered.

"There's no doubt that God sent you to help me," said Riley. "It's my guess He's got bigger things planned for you."

Tony turned and started for the truck. It was almost as if he were in a daze. He had spent all his life looking out for nobody but himself. This was his first experience at helping someone else, and it felt good. It felt real good.

Tony climbed into the truck and started the engine. He turned to Rinehart, who was quietly staring out the window. He glanced at Belva. He noticed that she had a slight hint of a smile.

CHAPTER FOUR

A young and pretty nurse by the name of Agnes stepped into the room while we were talking and asked us to leave. She said something about having to do something to Eddie. Seeing as how neither one of us wanted to witness whatever that something was, the bishop and I excused ourselves and stepped out into the hallway.

"This Tony fellow appears to be quite a colorful character," said Bishop Livingston. Then, suddenly, he turned to me with a look of surprise. "Oh, let me apologize for such an offensive remark."

I laughed aloud in an attempt to ease the man's guilt. "No offense taken, and, yes, he was a very colorful young man, a bit brassy and somewhat verbose, but his heart was always in the right place."

"I don't mean to sound rude or impatient, but could we continue with your story?" asked the bishop.

"Only if I can call him Eddie. That's been his name for the last forty years."

"Sure, fine. If that's what you want," said the bishop.

We found two chairs in the hallway and took a seat. Up until that time, I hadn't been sure if the bishop was truly interested in my story, but now that doubt was put to rest.

I turned towards the bishop and found him already on the edge of his chair. I smiled, cleared my throat and continued with my story.

"The next morning brought sunshine and a blue sky. The last remnants of winter were almost gone and the promise of summer grew even stronger.

It was just after seven when Tony and Eddie hit the sidewalk on their way to the diner. Not much had been said since the Frank Bower incident. Tony pretty much figured that Eddie hadn't approved of what he had done and was giving him the silent treatment. Of course, that didn't seem likely since Eddie seemed to be the type who would come right out and tell you what's on his mind.

Tony was not real sure if he was in trouble or not. He had seen his mother stay quiet for days at a time when she was depressed or mad about something, but he had never seen a man remain quiet for that long. They were just in front of the diner when Eddie came to a stop. He turned to Tony and gently placed a hand on his shoulder.

"What you did for that Amish family yesterday was highly commendable. I was wrong when I advised to stay out of it. In fact, I should have joined you. As of late, I have questioned my motives and have found that fear had prevailed. I guess I was afraid of confronting Frank

Bower and his bully friend. I have now learned that fear should not prevent me from doing the right thing. You did the right thing, and for that I am grateful to you."

This turned out to be a very intimate moment that Eddie had shared with Tony. I seriously doubt he had ever openly admitted doing wrong in his whole life. He turned to Tony with a sober almost despondent look on his face hoping for a few encouraging words.

With a straight face, Tony looked him right in the eyes. Suddenly, a big smile spread across his face. "Does this mean I can call you Eddie?"

Humility quickly turned to anger. "No, it does not," said Eddie. "You're still a smart ass kid who…"

Tony grabbed Eddie by the shoulder and led him to the door. "Stop jawin', will ya Eddie? I'm really hungry."

The two men pushed open the front door. The place grew silent as all eyes turned to them. It was a defining moment for Tony. He knew that this crowd of rednecks had heard about his confrontation with Frank Bower, but he wasn't quite sure how they would react. They stood there for what seemed like an eternity until one lone soul began to slowly clap his hands. Another joined in and before you knew it, the whole room was filled with applause.

The two men started for the table. As always the head of the table was left vacant for Eddie. Merle Lingo was sitting in the spot that Tony had occupied the previous day. He picked up his plate and coffee and moved to another spot.

"Some kind of boy, ya got there," said Willard.

"Ain't nobody ever kicked Buddy's ass," said Earl Bass. "And that's a fact."

Cletus slugged his open hand with his fist. "Wish I'd been there. I'd have hurt Buddy really bad and then I'd have tied into Frank."

"Knock it off, Cletus," said Fred Munson. "I heard that Clara Butts gave you a black eye once."

"That was back in the first grade," said Cletus.

"Here she comes now, Cletus," said Fred. "Wanna get even for that black eye thing?"

Clara stopped beside Eddie and leaned over. "Breakfast is on the house for you two today. What will you have?"

"I'll have the usual," said Eddie.

"And I'll have whatever he's having," said Tony.

Clara scribbled notes on a grease-stained pad and disappeared into the kitchen.

"Wow, Eddie," said Earl. "I think Clara has the hots for you."

Willard leaned closer to Eddie. "Is it true that you sat in the truck while Mr. Franko confronted Frank and Buddy?"

"You heard wrong," blurted Tony giving Eddie a quick glance. "Eddie here wanted to go toe-to-toe with Buddy, but I wanted him to keep an eye on Frank. I felt better knowing that Father Rinehart had my back."

Tony turned and found a glint in Eddie's eyes and for the first time the slightest sign of a smile.

"Say, Eddie," said Willard. "Mr. Franko here is dressed like a priest, then how come we don't address him as Father Franko?"

A big smile spread across Tony's face as he turned to Eddie. "Yeah. Why is that?"

"Mr. Franko is not an ordained priest," said Eddie.

"Sounds like we're splittin' hairs here," said Willard.

"I think we should call him Father Franko," said Fred Munson. "What do you think, Eddie? We'll call him Father Franko and call you Eddie."

It was about that time that Clara dropped off breakfast for Eddie and Tony. She leaned over and smiled at Tony. "Would there be anything else, Father Franko?"

Quiet laughter spread down the length of the table.

"That will be all," he said.

"Yes, sir," said Fred. "I think you've been replaced, Eddie."

"How are you at giving a sermon?" asked Cletus.

"Yeah," said Eddie with a big smile that no one had seen in years. "How are you at conducting a service?"

"Oh, I can hold my own," said Tony.

"Well, who would have guessed it?" said Eddie sipping his coffee. "Can't wait until I get the opportunity to listen to you."

"I'll see what I can do to pass along a few pointers," said Tony. "Unless I miss my guess, you've got to be a real sleeping aid."

Eddie bristled and sat straight in his chair. "How can you say something like that? You've never heard me preach."

"Come on, Eddie," said Cletus. "Listen to the boy. Trust me. You could use a few pointers."

"Cletus, the only reason you sleep through my sermons is because you're at the bar all night long the night before," said Eddie.

It was about that time that the front door opened and in walked Otis Hicks. He had the dangdest smile I had ever seen on his otherwise blank face. He walked over to the table and took a seat next to Bill Ballinger who was one of Eddie's most treasured friends. To be heard over the loud talking in the room, Otis had to shout, and believe me everyone listened this one time to Otis Hicks.

"Guess who I thought I saw just a minute ago down by the hardware?" he said with that smile that made his face look uglier the bigger it got. Now remember Otis was not the sharpest tool in the shed, so when he said guess who he saw, he absolutely meant it.

The room had become silent. The only sounds that could be heard were the forks scraping against the porcelain. Everyone knew that Otis wouldn't give up until at least one person guessed, so they took advantage of the opportunity to finish their already cold breakfasts.

"No, really. Somebody guess who I thought I saw."

"The queen of England," blurted Fred Munson.

"Oh, what would she be doing in a small town like this?" said Otis. "Somebody guess again."

Earl Bass stopped eating long enough to slightly turn his head to Otis. "Tell us who you thought you saw," he said with a commanding voice.

"Marie Sue Porter," blurted Otis.

For a brief few moments, the diner froze in time. Forks with food stopped in mid-air, mouths left gaping open. All eyes turned to Eddie.

"What did you say?" asked Eddie.

Otis frowned. "I said..."

"We heard you," said Cletus turning to Eddie with a look of concern.

Eddie fell back into his chair. He had a dazed look on his face.

"You know what that means, Eddie," said Willard. "She must have a twin."

"We all knew she would come back to haunt you," said Earl. "It was just a matter of time."

"Leave him alone, you guys," said Fred. "Let him enjoy his fantasies. Don't forget she was the hottest girl in school. While all you guys were dating blow up dolls, this guy was going out with the real thing."

Tony stared at the expressionless face of Eddie. He leaned closer and whispered, "Are you okay?"

Eddie snapped back to life. He pushed his plate away and pulled his coffee closer. "I'm fine. Why do you ask?"

"Tell me," said Tony. "Who is this Marie Sue Porter?"

"Yeah, Eddie," said Cletus. "Tell him the story."

Eddie cleared his throat. "She was just a friend of mine back in high school."

"Don't let him kid ya," said Cletus. "They were the hottest couple in school. Everyone was taking bets when they would get married."

"What happened?" asked Tony. "Why didn't you get married?"

Eddie paused for a moment. Everyone in the room stopped to see if he would answer the question. Finally, he got to his feet and started for the door. "Come on, boy," he said. "It's time you met Larry Joseph."

Tony caught up with Eddie outside the diner. He was walking at an unusually fast pace and had a sober almost worried look on his face.

"I don't think I want to go see this Larry Joseph guy," said Tony.

"Why do you say that?"

"From everything I've heard, he must be a bad man."

"On the contrary," said Eddie. "He's one of the most compassionate, caring men I know."

"I've heard nothing but bad things."

"Oh, I didn't say he wouldn't be tough to work for. In fact, many have tried and failed. Besides, wasn't Larry Joseph the reason the bishop sent you here?"

"I'm sure the bishop wouldn't mind if…"

"I'll have Wanda drive you out there," said Eddie. "Yes, I'm sure the bishop would want this."

As usual, Wanda had her day already planned, and hauling Tony out to Larry Joseph's wasn't a part of it. Even though it was only a two-mile ride to Joseph's, Wanda made certain that Tony knew how much of an inconvenience he had created for her.

"It ain't my fault," said Tony as he bounced along in the passenger's seat of the truck. "I have a driver's license and could have driven myself."

"And what did you expect us to do for transportation?" asked Wanda.

"That's not my problem."

Wanda shot Tony a quick look. "Land's sakes, how does that man put up with you? You surely have one nasty mouth."

"Hey, I don't want to go out here in the first place."

"You try talking like that to Mr. Joseph, and you'll find yourself elsewhere. Ain't likely he's gonna put up with the likeness of you anyhow."

"Come on, Wanda," said Tony. "It's just you and me here. Tell me the truth. These people around just don't like colored folk."

Wanda pulled the car over to the side of the road and stopped. "Don't you start with that racial stuff around here. That might have worked back there in the city, but these folks around here are good people. They deserve your respect until otherwise. You're damn lucky they let you live here like they do. After all, your story about the bishop sending you here is mighty lame at best. My guess is you're on the run from the law or some such thing as that. You best mind your manners, or I'll see to it that they run your butt out of town. You got that?"

"Yes, ma'am."

"Now when you get out here at Mr. Joseph's, you'd best be as good as you can be. Most white folk will put up with a lot and just sorta turn the cheek if you get what I'm saying. Most run across some smart-ass kid like you and simply chalk it up to the stupidity of youth. Mr. Joseph ain't that way. Unless you change your ways real fast, he will run your ass off his place. Chances are, he won't have to. You'll wanna get away from him as fast as you can."

"Sounds charming," said Tony with a bit of sarcasm in his voice.

"Mr. Joseph is one of the finest men I've ever know," she said pulling back onto the road. "You don't deserve to breathe the same air, so don't you dare shame me."

"Will I be allowed to say anything at all?"

"Speak when spoken and do whatever he tells you to do," said Wanda. "If you do what I tell you, you might make it to the end of the day."

She turned off the road and drove up a long and winding dirt road. It took them to a partial clearing and a half-built log cabin and a nearly completed barn. She stopped the truck and gazed at the surroundings.

"Seems to me you know quite a bit about things around here," said Tony.

"I know more than you think I do."

"You sound like some kind of a God around here," said Tony.

Wanda turned and looked Tony in the eyes. A smile spread across her face that was unnerving to him. For the rest of his life, he never forgot that particular moment.

"You'd be surprised," she simply said.

A big man with broad shoulders and huge arms stepped out of the barn and headed for the cabin. He glanced over at the truck and kept going.

"Good Lord, nobody told me he was a monster," said Tony.

"He's a big man," said Wanda. "That's for sure. But he's got a heart as gentle as a lamb."

Tony paused as he watched the man walk across the yard. Tony opened the door of the truck. "You coming back for me?"

"It's only two miles. If I'd had it my way, you'd have walked, but I'll be back around five."

Tony got out of the truck and watched as Wanda drove away. He turned to see Larry with a tool in one hand and bent over the end of a log.

"Hi," he said thrusting out his hand. "My name is Tony Franko."

Larry smiled one of his famous big smiles, the kind that would make his eyes disappear. "Larry Joseph," he said taking his hand. "I thought we already had a priest around these parts."

"That would be Father Rinehart," said Tony. "I'm a priest in training."

Larry returned to working on the log. "What brings you all the way out here," he said without looking up.

"I was sent here to help you."

Larry stopped what he was doing and stood straight. "Help me do what?"

"I don't know," said Tony. "Whatever you're doing out here with these log thingies."

"Who sent you?"

"The bishop."

"Why?"

"I don't know," said Tony. "I guess he figured you needed help."

Larry leaned back over the log he was working on. "You made a wasted trip."

"Why's that?"

"I don't want any help."

"What are you talking about? Everyone needs a little help."

"Not me."

"You're just about as stubborn as they said you were."

"Who said I was stubborn?"

"Just about everyone in town."

Larry grinned when he heard that remark. He picked up the log he was working on, shouldered it and started for the construction site.

"I can't believe you don't want my help," said Tony following behind.

"I can't believe you're still here," said Larry. He set the log in its place on the half-finished wall.

"You don't have to get nasty about it," said Tony backing away.

Larry said nothing. He kept on working as if Tony was not even there.

"Actually, it's almost as if you are insulting the bishop. He cared enough to send me down here to help, and you up and refuse. It's almost as if you looked the bishop right in the eyes and told him no thanks. Not that I was all that thrilled with the idea in the first place. After all, you're not the friendliest person in the world. I don't know who in their right mind would want to work with you. To tell you the truth, my time is more valuable than to waste it out here in the middle of nowhere. I'm a mover and a shaker. Do you know what I mean?"

Larry kept on working. It was if he had completely tuned Tony out, and now that I think about it, he probably had. Unfortunately, that didn't slow up Tony. He kept right on talking.

"If you don't mind my asking," said Tony. "Why are you building a log house way out here? You and the missus plan to live out here? You must have one mighty fine wife because I don't think there are that many women who would live out here in a dump like this."

Larry grimaced, took a deep breath and went back to work. "Anybody ever tell you that you talk too much," he said without looking up.

"Actually, I can't believe it myself," said Tony. "I can't seem to shut up. I don't normally talk this much, but for some reason I keep going on and on."

"Just my luck," muttered Larry.

Tony paused as he stared at Larry. The smile disappeared from his face. "You don't much care for me, do you?"

Larry turned and started for another log with Tony in pursuit.

"It's because of the color of my skin, isn't it?" asked Tony.

Larry picked up one end of a log and examined it. "Why? Is there something wrong with it?" asked Larry.

"It's not white, and that bothers you, doesn't it?"

"I hardly think it should be white seeing as how you're a Negro and all."

Tony shook his head. "See, there you go with that Negro stuff. It's the sixties, man. They call us black now."

"Oh, they do," said Larry. "So, Negro isn't in the dictionary anymore. Is that what you're saying?"

"No, it's still there just like the word Caucasian. Negro and Caucasian are technical names. We don't call you people Caucasians, we call you whites. So, why not call us blacks?"

Larry smiled. "You've got a good point there, but I still don't want your help."

"It's because I'm black, isn't it? Some dumb ole black boy from Detroit couldn't possibly know anything about work."

"Boy, you sure have a chip on your shoulder."

"Now you've gone and done it," said Tony. "I knew you'd get there eventually."

Larry picked up another log and started for the construction site with Tony tagging along.

"Do you want to know what you said this time?"

Larry dropped the log into place. "Not particularly."

"You called me boy. That's what you did."

"Well, aren't you?"

"You don't call a black man a boy."

"You couldn't be a day over twenty-one."

"Man, you just don't get it, do you? You're just another redneck who hates niggers."

Larry stopped and for the first time turned to face Tony. "You know, Mr. Franko, you come here onto my land, and it seems like all you've done is try to pick a fight. To make matters worse, you're now calling me names. I told you from the get go that I didn't want your help, now I'm telling you to get off my land."

"Sure. Fine," said Tony. "That's the last time I'll ever offer to help somebody." He remained unflinchingly staring at Larry.

"Well, what are you waiting on?" asked Larry.

"You're giving me a ride back into town, aren't you?"

Larry turned and walked away. "It's only two miles," he muttered. "The walk will do you good."

***

It was late morning when that young man opened the back door of the parsonage. Two miles for most any farm boy was a piece of cake, but for a city kid like Tony, it seemed more like a death march than anything else. Eddie was sitting at the kitchen table with a cup of coffee when Tony walked in.

"Good Lord, what happened to you?" asked Eddie.

Exhausted and sweat dripping down his face, Tony dropped into one of the kitchen chairs. "I walked all the way from Mr. Joseph's place."

Eddie smiled. "That's only two miles."

"That's what I'm talking about. It was a trip from hell…if you'll pardon the expression."

"You kids up there in Detroit must not do much walking."

"We don't do it out in the middle of nowhere under a blazing sun."

"Mr. Franko, do you ever stop whining?"

"Huh?"

Eddie shook his head in frustration. "Never mind," he said. "What are you doing back here so soon?"

"He threw me off his property!"

"Who did?"

"That Joseph guy," said Tony. "He told me to leave."

Eddie smiled. "That's not a surprise."

"Why didn't you tell me about this guy? He didn't want my help and flat out wouldn't let me help him."

"Hey, you're the one who came here with the sole purpose of helping Larry Joseph."

"I wouldn't spit on him if he were on fire."

"You mustn't say that," said Eddie. "He's a good man and deserves our respect."

"I think his problem is he's a bigot and is prejudiced against my kind."

Eddie leaned forward. "You know sometimes I think you're one of the nicest and smartest kids I've ever met, and then you go and say something like that."

"Besides all that, he's not a very nice man."

"How would you know?" asked Eddie. "You weren't there long enough to even remember his name. Besides, you have a mission this morning."

"A mission? What the…"

"Belva Bowdry wants to see you."

"What?"

"She called over here asking for you."

"Why on earth would that old woman want me?"

"I've been asking myself the same question."

"Don't I get anything to eat around here?"

"Go see Miss Bowdry, and you can have some lunch when you get back."

Tony slowly got to his feet. "That's five blocks, and I'm near death from walking two miles. Let me borrow the truck. I promise to keep it under fifteen."

"No chance."

"Then I refuse to go see Belva."

"Alright, alright," said Eddie. "But if anything happens to that truck…"

Tony dashed out the door. "Don't worry. It's in good hands," he cried out.

Tony did live up to his promise. He drove very slowly and very cautiously the five blocks to Belva's place. He parked at the curb and walked up the steps to the porch. Tony was more than a little curious as to why this old woman wanted to see him, but as he got closer to the front door his curiosity faded to more sobering thoughts of doom and gloom. This was an old woman living in an old house. For whatever reason she wanted to see a young black kid from Detroit couldn't be good.

Tony knocked on the door and stepped back. Moments later, the lock turned and the door opened just enough to allow a short, slightly bent over woman to peek out.

"Oh, it's you," she said then retreated back into the darkness of her house.

Tony stepped inside. "You wanted to see me?" he asked.

It was a dark, almost ominous looking interior with window shades covering boarded up windows. In one corner of the room next to a sofa, a small table lamp was lit. It cast a dingy yellow light across the floor.

"What's your name again?" she asked.

"Tony."

"Oh, yeah. Go sit over there," she said pointing at a lone armchair.

As Tony's eyes adjusted to the dark room, many things he hadn't seen before began to appear. As he approached the ragged chair, he noticed two cats lying on it. It was about that time that he noticed strange movement in all corners of the room.

"How many cats do you have?" he asked.

"Oh, I don't know," she said with a disgruntled voice. "I lost track after thirty."

Tony stood there staring helplessly at the two cats.

"Just push the black one off, and the other one will follow," she said.

Tony bent over and cautiously reached for the animal. It suddenly rolled over, raised a paw in a defensive move and hissed violently at him. Tony jumped and turned to Belva. "I don't think…"

"Get out of that chair!" screamed Belva as she thumped a baseball bat on the floor. Two cats rose six inches off the chair and disappeared instantly.

"It would seem they listen to you," said Tony.

"Every once in a while, I send one of 'em sailing across the room," she said. "Keeps 'em on their toes."

"Or paws," muttered Tony.

"Huh?"

"Nothing."

Belva leaned back in her chair. "Now what did you want?"

"You sent for me. Remember?"

"Oh, yeah. That's right," she said and reached for a sealed envelope that was on the table next to her. She handed it to Tony. "If anything should ever happen to me, I want you to give this envelope to my son."

Tony studied the envelope. The name Lloyd was written on the front. "What is it?"

"That's none of your business."

"Why me?"

"Why not?"

"You said you didn't like me," said Tony. "Didn't you say that?"

"I said I didn't like you," she said. "That doesn't mean you can't be trusted."

Tony paused for a moment to determine if what he heard was a compliment. "Why don't you give it to him yourself?"

"We haven't spoken to one another in five years."

"Why not?"

"Again, that's none of your business."

"You're kind of snippy for someone who is always needing favors," said Tony.

"Are you going to help me or not?"

"Yes, I'll help you. Don't know why seeing as how you're so mean," he muttered.

"I'm not mean," she barked. "Well, I suppose I sometimes seem that way. There are days when I just can't help myself."

Tony paused for a moment to consider his next question. "This all has something to do with your husband, doesn't it?"

She turned and smiled at Tony, a sad smile to be sure. "You're a very perceptive young man."

"I don't mean to pry, Mrs. Bowdry."

She closed her eyes and a warm smile spread across her face. "We were childhood sweethearts, you know. We were destined to be together even back then. All the kids in school said we were meant for each other, and that was over fifty years ago. It was a hard life at times. I guess we were no different than anybody else. There were good times and bad. Seems to me that God throws the bad times in there just to test you, to see how strong your faith in Him really is. Well, just about five years ago, God threw a nasty curve at us. Buford was diagnosed with cancer, and it wasn't more than a month or two later, he was gone."

Belva paused as she tried to collect herself. She turned her head to the floor. Taking deep breaths, she pulled out a hankie and wiped her eyes. I don't suppose there has been anything else in this world that could make that woman lose control of her emotions. She was as hard a woman as there is, but losing Buford was the hardest thing she ever had to endure.

"It still hurts," she muttered as she continued to wipe her eyes.

They say God moves in mysterious ways, and why He brought these two people together was puzzlement to me. At least in the beginning it was a mystery, but it soon became obvious that they were about to in some way help each other.

"I'm sorry," muttered Tony, half-attempting to lay his hand on her shoulder.

Belva straightened herself and took another deep breath. "Until the day we learned Buford was sick, we never knew a thing about cancer and what goes on. The day that the doctor came into Buford's room and explained about treatments, chemo whatever-its-called, and all the other stuff that goes along with that horrible killer was the worst day of my life. I knew he was in a hurry. Probably had an operation or some such to get to. I remember he stood there rattling the keys in his pocket as he blurted the options we had.

"Buford had no doubts at all what he wanted to do. Without any discussion, he decided to not take the treatments. The one thing that Buford did learn is the evil bastard was going to get him when it was all said and done. As far as he was concerned, he wanted to live out the few days he had left in a natural way and go find out from God why He was in such an all fired hurry to bring Buford home. You see, when it came to dying, Buford always said that he had his bags packed. He always figured that there was no reason to fuss about it. When his Master called for him, he would be ready."

She paused a moment then pointed at the letter in Tony's hand. "That there is the only unfinished business that I have left, and if you will be good enough to give that letter to my son, I'd appreciate it."

Tony tapped the top of his hand with the letter. "So, what does your son have to do with all this?"

"Never mind," she muttered.

"You've already told me some of the most intimate details of your final days with Buford. Why not tell me about your son?"

Belva got to her feet and started for the door. "Come on. It's time for you to leave."

"You're kicking me out of your house?"

"It's time for you to leave."

"I don't believe it," said Tony getting to his feet. "You ask for a favor then throw me out of your house."

"I'm a recluse," she said opening the front door. "I don't like people, and I certainly don't like..."

"Yeah, I know," said Tony. "I've heard it before. You don't like me."

Tony stepped out on the porch, and before he could turn around and say good bye, he heard the door slam shut and the deadbolt slide into place.

Remember back a ways when I told you that God put these two together for a reason? Belva would realize a benefit from the relationship in due time, but whether he believed it or not, Tony had already been blessed by this relationship. For the first time in his young life, he was concerned about someone else besides himself. When Tony stepped off Belva's porch, he was determined to reunite Belva and her son. He wasn't quite sure how or more importantly why he was going to do this, but he just knew he had to.

Tony raced home even topping the speed limit a few times. He parked at the back of the parsonage and nearly ran up the walk and into the house. Wanda was setting lunchmeat and bread on the table.

"Wanda, do you know where Belva Bowdry's son lives?" he asked taking a seat at the table.

"Lloyd lives out on Dry Lane Road," she said. "Why?"

"What kind of guy is he?"

"A farmer and a bit stubborn."

"That's not a surprise," muttered Tony.

"Huh?"

"Did you know they haven't spoken in five years?"

"I didn't know it had been that long."

"Do you know what happened?"

Wanda took a seat at the table. "As I recall, it had something to do with giving treatments for the cancer."

"That's what I thought," muttered Tony.

"You're thinking about getting those two back together again, aren't you?" asked Wanda.

Tony smiled. "It crossed my mind."

"And why would you want to go and do something like that?"

Tony thought for a moment. "To tell you the truth, I don't know."

"It's a new experience for you, isn't it?"

"What's that?"

"Doin' for others," she said. "You're not used to that, are you?"

Tony paused again. "I guess not."

"Feels good, doesn't it?"

"Wait a minute," blurted Tony as if he had awakened from a sleep. "How do you know so much?"

Wanda smiled and got to her feet.

"No, seriously. There's something about you that…"

It was about that time that Eddie walked in the room. "Ah, Wanda. We're not having baloney again, are we?"

"Perfect timing, Eddie. I have a question for you," said Tony.

"Will you stop calling me Eddie? It's Father Rinehart to you."

"Have you ever noticed that Wanda here sits on the sidelines acting like she hasn't a clue, and yet she's got a bead on everything that's going on?"

"She's a woman," said Eddie. "And women seem to have a sense for that kind of thing."

"In other words, they're nosey," said Tony.

"I prefer the way I put it, but…"

Wanda walked over and leaned over the table. "While you two nitwits are sitting here doing nothing, Frank Bower is giving another Amish family a rough time, and he ain't about to let the water flow down to their farms either."

"See what I mean?" said Tony. "She never leaves this kitchen, and yet she knows all this stuff."

Eddie turned and bowed his head. "I need to pray for Mr. Bower."

Tony nearly jumped out of his chair. "Pray for him! Come on. He doesn't need a prayer. He needs his ass kicked."

"Where are we going?"

"We're going out to see Frank Bower."

"I don't think we should bother Mr. Bower."

Tony grabbed Eddie under the arm. "I don't know much about Jesus, but my guess is He would want you to help these poor Amish people."

"I don't think Jesus would want us to lose our own lives while doing it."

"Come on," said Tony. "We're going out there and do the right thing."

There's an old saying around this part of the country. If the house is bigger than the barn, the wife is in charge. Well, Frank's house was about half the size of the barn and all of the outbuildings. Not that any woman would ever put up with the likes of Frank. Oh, some tried. In fact, Frank was married twice. Everyone in town was betting how long the marriages would last. Since Frank was on his best behavior during the first one, it lasted nearly six months. I think Orville Butts won that bet. No one came close to winning the bet on the second marriage. She left Frank on their wedding night. I can only guess why that happened.

Frank always liked to think of his ranch as a fortress and his ranch hands as soldiers. He was a bit paranoid in that he always had a soldier stationed at the front door of his house. As luck would have it, Buddy Butler was guarding the front door when Eddie and Tony showed up. He got to his feet when he saw the two men get out of the truck.

"What do ya want?" asked Buddy standing firm and tall.

"Mornin', Mr. Butler," said Tony. "How's that leg of yours?"

Buddy shook his leg. "It's fine."

"You took quite a shot to the crotch," said Tony. "Doin' okay there?"

"Knock it off," whispered Eddie.

"That was a cheap shot," said Buddy. "You and I are gonna do round two, and that's where you're going to get hurt."

"Enough of the small talk," said Eddie. "Get your boss out here."

Just then, the front door opened and out stepped Frank, cowboy hat and all. "What do you boys want?" he asked.

Eddie smiled. "Mr. Bower, I wonder if we might have a word with you in private?"

"Do your talking from there," said Frank. "Now what do you want?"

"We want you to leave the Amish alone," blurted Tony.

"Father Rinehart, you need to teach your boy some manners."

Eddie cleared his throat and tried to stand a bit taller. "He maybe a bit forthright maybe even verbose, but he speaks the truth."

"Anything else?" asked Frank.

"Yeah," said Tony. "Tear out that dam of yours and let the water flow on down the creek."

"Is there anything else I can do for you today?" asked Frank.

"I don't know," said Tony. "I could use a cup of coffee. How 'bout you, Eddie?"

"Oh, good Lord," muttered Eddie.

"The only reason I don't tear you in half is my respect for Rinehart," said Frank. "Now the two of you get off my property."

"What about my coffee?" said Tony.

"Get!" said Frank, pointing at their truck.

"You certainly have a long way to go in the area of people skills," said Eddie climbing to the truck.

"Why? What did I do wrong?"

"You need to gently sway people into thinking your way. Ease them along. You were flat out rude. And that coffee thing."

Tony started the engine and pulled out onto the road. "Well, I figured he wasn't going to help us anyhow."

"Well, we gave it a try," said Eddie.

"Oh, I'm not finished with Mr. Bower. There has to be a way to get that water flowing again."

"I'm impressed," said Eddie with a smile.

"With what?"

"You're suddenly helping someone other than yourself."

"Must be the outfit I'm wearing. Besides, I'm still number one on my list. By the way, what do you know about Belva Bowdry's son?"

"Lloyd is a veritable pain in the...er, he is a most difficult person to deal with. Why do you ask?"

"Just wondering."

"You're going to try and get Belva and him back together again, aren't you?"

"I don't know. Why?"

"You're kinda new at this helping others thing," said Eddie. "Maybe you should start out by getting a cat down out of a tree. Taking on Frank Bower and Lloyd Bowdry is definitely at the deep end of the pool."

"Don't worry," said Tony. "I can swim with the best of them."

"We sure have to do something about that name of yours."

"What's wrong with my name?"

"Good Lord, it doesn't fit you. Tony Franko is Italian, and you're anything but Italian."

"Let me ask you something," said Tony. "What kind of guy do you think of when you hear the name Tony Franko?"

"That's easy," said Eddie. "I think of a greasy-haired…"

"No. That's not what I'm asking. I'm asking what type of guy comes to mind."

"I don't know. I guess a scrapper, a young man who knows how to get things done."

Tony held out his arms and smiled. "Well?"

Eddie didn't get a chance to say anything more about the subject. They had just parked in front of the parsonage to find Cooter Samples, the town marshal waiting for them.

No one in town was quite certain how Cooter ever got the job as marshal. He, in fact, had been the marshal for nearly thirty years. He was a simple man with little else to do in life but give out tickets to speeders and try to keep the kids in town out of trouble. Some had accused Cooter of being stupid. The fact was he had never finished high school, not that that was all that important. Many residents dismissed his lack of education saying how smart does a marshal have to be?

Cooter was paid only $25.68 per week. This was hardly enough to support even a single man, so Cooter much to the displeasure of his neighbors owned and maintained a junkyard. It was an unsightly mess in front of and nearly surrounding his house. It wasn't so much the sight and smell that upset his neighbors, as it was the fact that it was a haven for rodents especially rats. Since Cooter didn't believe in killing animals and, in fact, wouldn't even swat a mosquito, it was a healthy population of rodents that lived there thriving well from the garbage that was sometimes dumped there, and they multiplied at an alarming rate.

Cooter never did get married. Oh, he dated from time to time, but he could never find a woman who could adapt to such a lifestyle. I mean, after all, what woman wouldn't love spending time with a man who sometimes forgets his weekly bath and actually encourages the rats to come inside his house. He not only fed the little boogers but actually allowed them to sleep in his bed. Now these were only rumors you understand. No one had actually entered his house to verify the stories, but if you knew Cooter you knew there was a real good chance they were true.

"Morning, Cooter," said Eddie getting out of the truck.

"Morning, Father Rinehart."

"Fine day, isn't it?" asked Eddie.

All the time they're talking, Cooter is giving Tony the once over.

"So this is your assistant everybody is talking about."

"Cooter, this is Tony. Tony, this is Cooter."

"Glad to meet you," said Cooter taking Tony's hand.

"Likewise," said Tony.

"What brings you over to this side of town?" asked Eddie.

"I got a report that a young black male escaped from the prison," said Cooter.

"What's that got to do with us," said Eddie.

"Well, the funny thing is your new assistant here fits the description to a tee."

"That's absurd," said Eddie. "The bishop himself sent Tony here to help me. As you can clearly see from his garb, he's not a criminal."

"Yeah, well, I sent for a photograph of this guy," said Cooter. "Maybe then, we'll know for sure."

"That's some pretty heavy duty thinking, Cooter, my man," said Eddie. "Now be off with you. We've got work to do."

As they parted company, Eddie turned to Tony. Tell me you're not this escaped prisoner he was talking about."

Tony spread his arms wide. "Do I look like an escaped convict to you?"

"Well, I..."

"I need to borrow the truck," blurted Tony.

"What?"

"I'll only be gone for an hour."

"Didn't I tell you that you were never to drive that truck without me?"

"I think that's what you said."

Eddie slowly shook his head. "So you think that's what I said."

Tony climbed into the truck. "I'll be careful."

"What are you doing? I didn't say you could use it."

Tony started the engine. "I promise to stay under the speed limit."

"If anything happens to that truck..." said Eddie as he drove away.

***

Lloyd Bowdry was a big man, slow by some standards and retarded by others. For that reason and perhaps the fact that he always had snot hanging from his nose was why Lloyd lived alone. He explained it as a sinus condition beyond his control, and while no one disagreed with this explanation, it only served as more evidence that he was retarded.

He lived with his parents until he was nearly forty when his dad died. It was shortly after the funeral that he moved out. It was a shock to most of the townspeople. Here his mother had just lost her husband, a time when she needed Lloyd the most, and he up and moves out. Must have been something mighty important that came between them. Then again, I've learned over the years that most of the time it's something as simple as a misunderstanding or a slip of the tongue.

Tony drove across town and soon found himself out in the country all the time keeping his speed no more than twenty miles per hour. It pained him deeply to drive that slowly, but he was absolutely certain that someone would report him to Rinehart. He turned off the country road into a driveway and parked the truck. It was an old farmhouse in bad need of repair. He got out of the truck and knocked on the door.

The door opened slightly, and a face appeared. "Who are you?" asked Lloyd.

"My name is Tony Franko."

"Are you some kind of a priest or something?"

"I'm in training to be one."

"What the hell do you want?"

"I'd like to talk to you, if you don't mind," said Tony trying to squeeze through the opening.

Lloyd closed the door even tighter. "About what?"

"I'd like to talk to you about your mother."

"Go to hell," he said and closed the door.

Tony stood there for several moments just staring at the closed door. He then got back in his truck and drove away.

When he got back to the parsonage, Eddie was in his office with the door open. Tony drifted slowly into his office and with a stunned look on his face sat down near Eddie.

"How did it go with Lloyd?" asked Eddie.

"He slammed the door in my face."

Eddie chuckled. "Oh, what a surprise."

"Is it because I'm black?"

"No."

"Is it because I'm dressed like a priest?"

"No."

"Then what is it?"

"Let me guess," said Eddie. "You mentioned his mother, didn't you?"

"Well, yes, I did."

"Lloyd doesn't like talking about his mother to anyone especially a stranger. Now if you had mentioned something about food, he would have asked you in. Lloyd loves to eat."

Tony frowned. "Why didn't you tell me this before I went out there?"

"You didn't ask."

Tony paused for a moment then leaned forward as if to change the conversation. "When your local marshal showed up today, you defended me. Why did you do that?"

"What do you mean?"

"There was a time when you would have had me hauled away just on the chance I was that escaped convict. What changed your mind?"

At this point, Eddie blushed just a little bit and wore a sheepish smile. "I don't know," he muttered.

"You like me, don't you?"

"Huh?"

You can't hide behind that gruff exterior," said Tony. "You like the snotty black kid who came to live with you."

"That's not necessarily true."

"Yes, it is."

"I just need the extra help," said Eddie. "That's all."

"That's a lie, and you know it. You flat out told me you didn't need any help."

"Well, things have changed since then. Besides, what about you?"

"What about you?"

"You've changed since coming here."

"I have not. I'm still the simple smart ass I've always been."

"When you first came here, there was nobody in your radar but you. It was all about you, and now you're finding yourself helping others."

"You have a strong imagination, my friend," said Tony. "I ain't helping anybody in this hick town but myself. No way."

"What about the Amish families you've defended, and what about Belva Bowdry and her son?"

"Ah, anybody would have helped them under the circumstances."

"I was there, and I didn't," said Eddie. "Not that I'm proud of that."

"Enough talk about me," said Tony. "What about you? How did you get into this racket?"

"Oh, I don't know. The same as any other man of God, I guess. One day without warning God calls me to do His work."

"God called to you?"

"Yes."

"What did He say?"

"What do you mean?"

"What did God say to you when He called you. He had to have said something."

"God didn't talk to me as such," said Eddie. "It's a feeling, a very unmistakable feeling."

"And you had no doubt that it was God?"

Eddie smiled. "No doubts at all."

"Can't imagine," muttered Tony.

Eddie's smile disappeared. He had suspected something all along and now was the time to find the answer to a burning question. "You don't believe in God, do you?"

Tony paused for a moment. "You can't expect me to believe that some being made this earth and everything that goes with it. It's just too much for me to swallow. Can you honestly say that you understand how He did all this?"

"Oh, no," said Eddie. "I have no idea how He did it."

"Then how can you believe that this being called God created the heavens and the earth?"

Eddie smiled and slowly shook his head. "The arrogance of mankind," he muttered.

"What do you mean by that?" Tony asked.

Eddie turned to face Tony. "I know you think you have all the answers. You're no different than most humans. At one time or the other, we all think we have it figured out. Believe me, there was a time when I thought I knew it all. God didn't do us any favors when He designed the human brain. We may think we're the smartest animal on the planet and we might very well be, but in the big scheme of things we're only a couple notches above a snake or a slug. God gave us enough thinking power so that we can keep ourselves zipped up and keep from soiling ourselves. To tell you the truth, He wasn't all that sure we would accomplish that, so He gave us biological urges that warn us of an impending nasty biological function. I think He was concerned about our social graces."

"You certainly have a low opinion of the human race," said Tony.

Eddie leaned forward. "Don't think I'm being flippant about our lot in life, but it is a genuine fact that we have very limited thinking. Ask a doctor sometime what triggers the heart to start beating in an unborn fetus. He can't tell you because he doesn't know. Consider conception if you will. Two fluids mix together, and a human being is formed with bones, fluids, organs and a brain more complex than any computer ever thought of by man. There are so many intricate parts on a human designed not by chance or accident rather by a power much greater than we can ever comprehend. Einstein recently said that you must be a fool to not believe that thought went into all this." Eddie leaned in closer. "Did you know that at every joint in your body, there is a tiny little sac that secretes a lubricant that is far more slippery than anything man's has ever invented. We could have lived our lives without it, but because someone with far more brain power than us was concerned about the pain of bone on bone, He included that little unknown feature. The next time you cut yourself, look down on that bleeding wound and marvel at the miracle that soon happens. The body actually heals itself. What an incredible concept. You take such an event for granted, and yet it unfolds right in front of you. There are so many wondrous things in life that you miss, and even if you should recognize it you wouldn't understand it anyhow. Just the DNA in your body is probably the most remarkable thing in the universe. As you know or probably don't know, DNA is the formula or the plans if you will for assembling you. If you were to read those plans non-stop, it would take you ninety-six years, and those plans are contained within everyone of your cells."

"I never knew that…"

"Have you ever wondered what holds us together, my young friend? The thing that keeps us from melting into a pile of goo, is a molecule called laminin. Not many people have ever heard of laminin, but it's the glue that holds our molecules together. Want to know what it looks like? I was dumbfounded the first time I saw a picture of one. It was taken with the aid of an electron microscope and each and every one of them is in the shape of a cross. You see what God is trying to tell you? The cross is the universal symbol of Jesus Christ, and He put that sign of the cross within each of the cells in your body. It's a subtle sign. By all means, probably the most subtle sign of all, and yet the most powerful. God is telling you He is a part of you. He is at the very core of your being."

"I tell you all this, Tony, so that I can deliver to you the most important message of all. In spite of the fact that you don't believe in Him, He still loves you. He's got you right in the palm of His hand, and His promise to you is a big one. God promises that He will always be there for you, Tony. No matter what you do or say, He is right there to help you, and the only thing He asks of you is for you to just believe. That's it, Tony, plain and simple. Just believe. If you truly believe in God, He will take you places you never dreamed of.

Eddie grew silent. He knew he had said too much. Nobody wants a sermon and especially this young man from Detroit. His intentions were good, but Eddie doubted the impact he had had on Tony.

Tony turned to Eddie with a solemn look. "I don't disagree with what you have said. It was somewhat convincing. In fact, I liked the way you used something from the science community to help prove your convictions. I don't mind telling you I'd like to see one of those laminins myself. You haven't miraculously converted me, but I will think about what you said. I could tell you that I'm a born again Christian, but I think you'd know better."

Then Eddie said something. I'm not sure if he planned it, or it just happened. He moved closer and took one of Tony's hands and smothered it with both of his. He looked Tony in the eyes and said, "Tony, I believe in you. I think God has plans for you. I think you're going to do great things, maybe not the kind of great things most people think about. You're not going to be some great inventor or a leader of our country. I think you're going to make an impact on the lives of people. You're going to help people through difficult times and make their lives a little bit better, and what in this world is more important than that? God has a plan for you. I'm sure of that. The world is going to be a little bit better because Tony Franko was here."

Tony smiled. "Is that why you put up with my crap?"

Eddie smiled back. "That's why I put up with your crap."

CHAPTER FIVE

The nurse stepped out of Eddie's room. She smiled and told us we could return then walked away. I wasn't quite sure if the bishop was enjoying this or was simply being polite. Either way, it gave both of us something to do while we waited.

As we walked back into the room, I couldn't help but notice that Eddie seemed to have changed. Where before he had what appeared to be a slight smile on his face, he now wore a very distinct and even broad smile. I wasn't sure what that nurse had done to him, but I was quite sure that he didn't disapprove.

We both scooted our chairs closer to Eddie and sat back down. I glanced over at the bishop. It seemed that he was eager to hear more. We weren't going anywhere nor had much to do for that matter, so I picked up where I had left off.

"Now when I look back, it's clear that God put Tony and Eddie together for a reason. I think Eddie learned a lot from young Tony. In fact, I think he learned more than he even realized. But the real winner in the relationship was Tony. Being raised on the streets of Detroit and without any real parental guidance, he was forced to fend for himself. The idea of helping others wasn't a part of Tony's world. It was literally self-preservation in a world of cruelty and crime. Tony was now learning the joy of helping others, but I don't think God thought he was learning it fast enough. The next event that happened in Tony's life would change him forever, and there's no way you can convince me that God didn't have a hand in this.

It was started when Tony was walking uptown to get a few groceries for Wanda. Eddie was in one of his stubborn moods and wouldn't let him use the truck, so Tony was forced to walk. It's funny how things happen. If Tony had driven the truck, he never would have had his life changing experience.

Tony was four blocks from downtown when he heard a loud crash. It was unmistakably the sound of metal on metal. He ran to the next block and looked to his left. There less than a hundred feet away was the aftermath of and accident. Obviously, one car had run the stoplight and had broadsided the other. Metal and broken glass were strewn over the street and the curb where one of the cars had come to rest.

Tony scanned the scene looking for victims. His eyes fell on a young boy maybe four or five years of age. He was clutching his bloodied head and walking aimlessly off the curb and into the road. Now Tony might not have been the greatest baseball or football player alive, but he definitely was a fast runner. He nearly flew over the curb and into the street. Just as the boy was about to collapse, Tony scooped him up in his arms. He turned to a bystander. "Where's the hospital?" he asked.

"We don't have one," she said then pointed. But there's the doctor's office right over there about two blocks away."

Stilling holding the boy, Tony turned in that direction.

"It's a dark green building with a white picket fence. There's a sign on the front that says, Doctor Burns."

Tony took a deep breath and started running. He jumped over fences, ran through backyards, and across side streets. Tony's heart was breaking. He wanted to look down at the boy but was afraid of what he might find. The thought of that young boy dying in his arms made him run all the faster.

Just as Tony thought he couldn't run another step, the sign of Doctor Burns loomed in front of him over the door of a small green shingled house. Still holding the boy in his arms, he burst through the front door. Every seat in the waiting room was taken. The nurse behind the counter looked up in shock. Tony didn't wait for an invitation. He burst through the door that led to the examination room. A middle aged man with white hair and dressed in a white coat was bent over a sink washing his hands.

"Doc, we need your help," said Tony easing the boy onto a table.

Burns turned and stared at the blood-covered boy. He rushed across the room. "What happened?" he asked.

"Car accident," said Tony.

"Who is he?"

"Don't know, Doc. I was just passing by."

Burns took a soft cloth and gently soaked the blood from his face. "Why it's little Jimmy Bower."

"Any relationship to Frank?"

"It's his grandson," said Burns. "Now you go and get out of here. I have work to do."

Tony, reluctantly, trudged out into the hallway. He sat on a small wooden bench just outside Jimmy's room. Actually, Tony was in the way, what with the nurses rushing in and out of the room, but for some unknown reason Tony felt compelled to stay near Jimmy.

One of the nurses paused for a moment. "There's an empty chair in the waiting room, if you like," she said.

"No, thanks," said Tony. "I'm fine."

With that she shrugged her shoulders and went on about her business.

There were times when I regarded Tony Franko as one of the smartest kids around. Some would call him sharp as a tack, even gifted. Then there were times when it didn't seem as if he could remember his own name. I'll have to admit that this event was a bit different. Without doubt, Tony's mind had blotted out certain memories, memories that needed to be forgotten such as the one of his own brother dying in his arms. Unfortunately, that memory would haunt him the rest of his life. Maybe he'd feel differently if this little guy were to pull through and live. Then again, maybe it would just make the loss of his brother even more painful. Either way, he needed this little boy to survive.

Tony leaned back on the bench and took a deep breath. Seemed like he'd been there for hours even though he knew it had only been minutes. Nurses were coming and going into the room. He tried to convince himself that such activity was a good sign, but the distressed looks on their faces and the panic in their steps told him otherwise. He really shouldn't feel badly. After all, he was the one who picked the boy up and carried him two blocks to the doctor's office. Nobody else took the initiative, and there were plenty others standing around. He had more than done his share. No one would blame him if he got up and walked out with his head held high. After all, if it hadn't been for his quick actions, the boy might have died right there in the street. Yes, sir. He had done everything he could. That's for sure. He was just a mortal and not a very bright one at that. The rest was up to the doc and God. Tony thought about saying a little prayer for Jimmy. He wasn't sure how much good it would do, but it couldn't hurt. It would certainly be the right thing to do seeing as how he was a man of God...kinda. The only problem was he had never said a prayer. Throughout his whole life, Tony had never prayed to God. Even when the Butler brothers chased him down an alley to beat him up for slashing their bicycle tires, he didn't say a prayer. It wasn't that he was an atheist or anything like that, it's just that he had never been exposed to the church and what it meant to have God on your side.

Tony slid closer to the doorway and leaned over to hear the activity going on inside the room. There was quiet talk, too soft to understand. It was the kind of talk that came in short bursts of chopped-up sentences. A nurse appeared in the doorway. She buried her face in her hands as she stared back into the room. Somehow they knew. They knew it was time.

Above the confusion and muted voices there was the beeping sound from the heart monitor. It was an irritating sound but offered hope that things would turn out okay. For as long as that machine continued to chirp, it meant the patient was still alive. As I remember back, that beeping sound seemed to grow louder. As all activity came to a stop and everyone froze, the sound now overpowered the room. It had become a sharp, deafening noise that filled the room and the hallway. Everything and everybody had grown silent. All eyes turned to the monitor.

Then it happened. The bouncing ball of light on the monitor stopped. The repetitious beeping noise became a steady ear-piercing sound. Tony leaned over until he could see the monitor. The bouncing ball of light was now streaking across the bottom of the screen leaving no doubt as to the fate of the young boy lying in the bed. The nurse in the doorway blubbered. She buried her face in her hands and ran away. Tony stepped into the doorway in time to see the doctor remove his plastic gloves and throw them on the floor. He muttered an expletive, whispered instructions to the remaining nurse, and they then both left the room.

Tony stood in the open doorway. It was strangely silent in the room, an eerie silence that left Tony frozen in one spot. He stood there for several moments surveying the room and the now lifeless body of Jimmy Bower. Slowly and cautiously, he tiptoed across the room as if trying not to awaken someone and stopped at the side of the bed. The blood in the young boy's body had stopped circulating and was now settling where gravity deemed it. His eyes were closed; his mouth slightly open and his skin had already turned pale.

Tony picked up his lifeless hand. It was still warm. Tony held the small hand tightly within his and began to cry. It just didn't seem fair. Such a young and innocent life ended so casually and as if it were ordained or meant to be. Life was savagely ripped from this boy's body in a lonely, dark room on a day like any other day. It just didn't seem fair. Tony sniffled and wiped the tears from his eyes.

"I'm sorry," he said softly. "I couldn't have run any faster. I wish I could have. You might still be alive."

Tears gushed down his cheeks as Tony dropped to his knees. Still clutching Jimmy's tiny hand, Tony bowed his head. His heart was breaking. This couldn't be happening again. God surely wouldn't take another young, innocent soul.

"Dear God," he muttered aloud, his eyes focused upwards. "I know I don't deserve any breaks from you. I haven't exactly been the most perfect boy in the neighborhood. But what I'm asking for is not for my sake. I'm asking that you give this boy his life back. He was so young and innocent. He had his whole life in front of him. It just doesn't seem right. I know that I don't have any right to ask anything of you. Since I've never taken the time or effort to talk to you when things are good, why would you even listen to me when I ask for help?

"Since I moved here to this little town, I'm learning what it's like to help other, and to tell you the truth I think I kinda like it, not that I'm planning on becoming a priest or anything. No sir, that's not for me. As soon as the heat is off, I'm outta here. I will be headed back to Detroit. After all, that's where I belong."

Tony turned to the still body lying on the bed. He stared at Jimmy for several moments until a lone tear streaked down his face. "I'll tell you what," said Tony slapping his knee and looking upwards again. "I take it all back. You give Jimmy back his life, and I'll become a priest, plain and simple. That's the deal, take it or leave it."

You know, it's been said that God brings a deciding moment to everyone's life. These are pivotal moments that could possibly change your life forever. It could be a decision to be made that would take you down one road or another, or it could be a life-changing event. Tony was about to experience such an event that was not only life changing but could easily be considered a miracle.

He slowly got to his feet and just stood there staring at the lifeless body. As I think back, I really believe God was setting the stage. Just as he began to walk away, the flat line monitor came to life. The tiny ball of light was now bouncing across the screen. Tony reached down and grabbed the boy's hand. The small fragile fingers twitched uncontrollably. Color returned to his face and body as he slowly squirmed on the table. Tony wasn't sure if he should scream or run for help. Instead, he decided to stay and watch this miracle unfold before his very eyes.

Suddenly, the young man's eyes opened. He stared into Tony's eyes, his face without expression. Then slowly and without any warning, his face melted into a smile.

"Hi," he muttered.

"Hi, yourself," said Tony.

The young boy glanced around the room. "Where am I?"

"You're in the doctor's office."

"What happened?"

Before Tony could answer, two nurses and a doctor exploded into the room.

"Good Lord!" shouted one of the nurses. "He's alive."

They huddled around him, one feeling his pulse and another reconnecting tubes and such. Frankly, I never saw anyone in the field of medicine move quite that fast. They were so busy and caught up in the moment, I don't think anyone of them had time to absorb what had just happened. They scrambled to aid this human being who had either returned from the dead or had not actually died in the first place. Either way, they were focussed on providing him with every means of available support.

Tony drifted back to give them room to work. The poor fella kept stepping backwards until he hit the wall. He was so dumbfounded that all he could do was stare at the people who were frantically working to save the young boy. He had this huge cockeyed smile on his face, and he was babbling something that nobody could understand.

Doc Burns stepped back from the others and turned to Tony. "What did you do to this boy?" he asked very abruptly.

"Huh?" muttered Tony.

"This boy was clinically dead now what did you do to him?"

Tony slowly glanced at the boy who by now was nearly sitting up then turned back to Burns. "Said a prayer," he softly uttered.

"You did what?"

"I said a prayer."

"What kind of prayer? What did you ask for?"

"I simply asked God to bring him back to life. It was that simple. Nothing fancy about it. The best part is it worked."

Burns turned to Jimmy then back to Tony. "Did you touch him in any way?"

"No."

"You didn't slap him or poke him somewhere?"

"No," said Tony.

"And all you did was say a prayer over him?"

"That's all."

Burns paused for a moment as if he was trying to take it all in. "That must have been one powerful prayer," he said and turned back to Jimmy.

With a dazed look that was even greater than before, Tony wandered out of the room and into the hallway. Unfortunately, it was just about the time that Frank Bower was marching down the aisle. Someone told him that his grandson had been killed in a car accident. Enraged and frantic to learn the truth, Frank nearly flew to the doctor's office. He stormed through the front door and literally ran into Tony.

"What are you doing in here?" Frank asked.

Tony was still wearing a big smile and still in a daze. "I was…"

"Were you in my grandson's room?"

"I was…"

"I'd better never catch you in there again!"

Tony simply ignored Frank and began to walk away. It was as if Frank didn't even exist.

"If I find out that you so much as touched my grandson…" Frank never finished his warning, because Tony had already opened the door and walked out of the office.

***

Wanda draped a dishcloth over a pile of clean dishes. She poured herself a cup of coffee and sat down at the table. "Wish I had a nickel for every dish I ever washed," she said with a sigh.

From across the table, Father Rinehart set down his cup. "Then you'd be so rich, you wouldn't have anything to do with me."

"Land sakes, I'd sure enough like to prove you wrong," said Wanda. "But I ain't holding my breath 'til it happens."

Now somewhere between the doctor's office and the parsonage, Tony came out of his stupor, because when he hit the door it was as if his tail was on fire.

"Father Rinehart!" he shouted as he took a seat at the table.

"Father Rinehart?" he asked. "What happened to Eddie?"

"You're not gonna believe what just happened."

"Try me."

"It was a miracle."

"What was a miracle?"

"I just performed a miracle."

Eddie grabbed him by the arm. "Slow down, Tony and tell me what happened."

Tony took deep breaths. "Little Jimmy Bower was in an accident."

"Oh, my," said Eddie. "Is he okay?"

"I carried him to Doc Burns office where they were working on him when the next thing you know, poor little Jimmy up and died."

"Are you sure he's dead?"

"That's where the miracle came in, because I brought him back to life."

"What are you talking about?"

"The little ball on the monitor went flat line, and everybody slowly walked away. I heard one of the nurses say he was dead. Well, I walked over to him, and sure enough he looked dead alright. I've only seen a couple dead people in my life, but there was no doubt about whether or not that boy was dead."

"Well, what did you do?" asked Eddie leaning forward in his chair.

"For the very first time in my life, I said a prayer."

"You've never prayed before?"

"Not before today."

"I'd think anybody living in Detroit would be praying everyday," said Eddie.

"No, sir. This was my first one."

"Must have been a powerful prayer," Eddie said.

"All I did was to ask God if He would let him live," said Tony. "The next thing I knew that monitor lit up with the bouncing ball, and Jimmy started to move. To tell you the truth, it scared me to death. Caught me by surprise, that's for sure. I never expected God to make good on a request like that."

"Is he still alive?" Eddie asked.

"He was when I left."

Eddie turned away with a smile. "I don't believe it," he muttered.

"Oh, you'll believe it when you see little Jimmy," said Tony.

"No, it's not that," said Eddie. "I've been praying all my life, and I can't really say for sure that God ever answered even one prayer."

"If you're real nice to me, I might give you a few tips."

"So, where do you go now?" asked Eddie in an effort to avoid Tony's last comment.

"What do you mean?"

"You saw God's handiwork," said Eddie. "You actually saw a miracle performed by God. What are you going to do about it?"

The smile disappeared from Tony's face. "Well, sure it was a miracle, and I'm happy for Jimmy."

Eddie stood and began to pace the floor. "You don't think that miracle happened for the benefit of little Jimmy, do you?"

"Well, it brought Jimmy back to…"

"You're missing the point here," said Eddie, his voice rising to a fever pitch. "God didn't perform that miracle for Jimmy's sake...He did it for you. What an awesome way to get your attention, to introduce Himself to you. This was God's wake up call to you. He has plans for you, son. Big plans. God doesn't normally operate like this. He doesn't do tricks and hocus pocus. You are destined to do something very important. All we have to do is figure out what that something is."

Tony intently listened to what Eddie had to say then grew silent as he tried to digest it all. "I don't think so."

"What do you mean by I don't think so?" Eddie asked.

"I think God used me to save that little boy. That's all. I just happened to be at the right place at the right time."

Eddie slowly shook his head. "Sometimes, I feel so sorry for you, my friend. You have no vision, no imagination. You need to trust in God. Believe that He has a purpose for you. Good Lord, let it happen. Where He is taking you has to be better than where you are right now."

"I wish I could believe you."

"Why are you fighting it?" Eddie asked. "The Supreme Being, the Master of the universe wants to help you. He wants to take you places you never dreamed of. Why can't you just trust in Him?"

Tony got to his feet. He had a sad if not discouraged look on his face. Then, as if he were thinking out loud, he muttered, "Where was God when my brother needed Him?"

"What?" asked Eddie.

"Never mind," said Tony starting for the door. "I'm going to give Lloyd one more try."

"Don't go there empty-handed," said Eddie. He turned to Wanda. "Wrap up that chicken that's leftover from last night. You're going to need all the help you can get."

Lloyd was sitting on the front porch when Tony pulled into his driveway. He picked up the package and started for the front of the house.

"What are you doing back here?" growled Lloyd.

Tony said nothing until he reached the porch. "Wanda wanted you to try her new recipe for fried chicken," he said as he handed him the paper bag.

It was if Tony had said some magic word. Lloyd jabbed his hand into the bag and found a drumstick wrapped in wax paper. "Oh, dear God," he muttered as he took a bite. "Ain't nobody can fix chicken like Wanda. She's the reason I go to the ice cream social every year. Can't get enough of her fried chicken. Ever taste it?"

"Can't say as I have," said Tony.

Lloyd took another bite of the chicken. "Don't get any ideas about this here chicken, 'cause it's all mine. Go talk to Wanda if you want to try it."

Tony stared at Lloyd as he devoured the food. "After watching you, I just might talk to Wanda."

"You know, that woman is a saint," said Lloyd dropping a chicken bone back into the bag. "I've noticed over the years I've known her, she ain't never done nothing wrong, and it seems to me that everything she does is far better than anybody else can do."

"She is a wonder at that," muttered Tony.

"Take this chicken for example. Ain't nobody can do better. Many have tried, and every last one of them has failed."

"Now that you mention it, there is something strangely unique about that woman," said Tony deep in thought.

"Tell Wanda the chicken was perfect as always," said Lloyd. "Actually, I'm not quite sure what she wanted because it tasted just like it always does."

"Well, I'll tell her it met your approval," said Tony.

The smile disappeared from Lloyd's face. "So, you didn't come all the way out here just to feed me. What's it this time?"

"Your mother is dying," blurted Tony.

Now I know Tony's mission was to get Lloyd's attention. Well, that one statement did the trick. Lloyd's feet crashed to the floor as he leaned forward nearly falling out of his chair.

"What?" asked Lloyd.

"She has the same cancer that killed your father."

"He died of prostrate cancer."

"Well, yes…that's right," said Tony. "This is the female version of it."

Lloyd's mouth dropped open as his face took on a somewhat puzzled look. "The female version…"

"She only has a short time left," said Tony. "Don't you think it's about time you two buried the axe?"

"Well, I suppose…"

"Just out of curiosity, Lloyd, what is this rift between the two of all about anyhow?"

Lloyd blushed and smiled sheepishly. "Actually, it really was nothing."

"Somehow I figured as much," said Tony. "So, what happened that split you two apart?"

Lloyd paused. He still had this sheepish look on his face because he knew how silly it would soon sound to an outsider. "She caught me smoking."

Tony smiled. "She caught you smoking."

"She caught me smoking, and a big fight broke out. The next thing I knew I was moving out of the house."

"I suppose you were a kid at the time," said Tony.

"Actually, I was 24 at the time."

"So, you were 24, and she wouldn't let you smoke. Did she give you any reason?"

"She didn't want me stinking up the house."

"So, there was a big fight."

"Yes."

"And you moved out."

"Sounds a bit stupid now that I think about it."

Tony jumped to his feet. "Come on. Let's go."

Lloyd followed, taking small steps. "Where are we going?"

"We're going over to your mother's place, and you're going to apologize."

"I'm not apologizing," said Lloyd. "She started it."

Tony stopped, turned and pointed a finger at Lloyd. "There is no way you're going to live with yourself if you don't fix this right here and now," said Tony with conviction. "Now get in the truck."

It was only a five minute drive from Lloyd's house to his mother's, but it seemed like an eternity. Tony was a bit nervous for having lied about Belva's eminent death. He wasn't quite sure how they would react once the truth came out. Of course, Lloyd was upset after having learned that he was losing his mother and was concerned about confronting her after all the time that had passed.

Tony pulled into her driveway and turned off the engine. For several moments, they both nervously stared at the house.

"Let's call it off," said Lloyd wringing his hands. "I changed my mind."

"Not a chance," said Tony. "You're going in that house and patch up this thing between you two."

Lloyd squared himself around in the seat facing Tony. He had a scowl on his face. "Do you think you're big enough to make me?"

Tony slowly turned to Lloyd with a confident smile that bordered on a sneer. "Yeah...yeah, I'm big enough. Now get out of the truck."

Tony could only hope that he was doing the right thing. After all, throwing them together could make things even worse, and if Lloyd discovers that Tony lied to him and that she isn't dying, there would be hard feelings for sure.

They stepped onto the porch, and Tony gently knocked on the door.

"I think I'll wait for you in the truck," said Tony turning away.

Lloyd grabbed him by the arm. "You're staying right by my side."

Just then, the door swung open with Belva standing in the doorway. "What do you two want?" she barked.

There was a long pause as the two men stood there dumbfounded. I'm most certain they both were wondering the same thing and was wishing they were someplace else.

"Well?" she demanded.

"Hi, Ma," said Lloyd. "I just stopped by to see how you're doing."

She turned to Tony. "What are you doing here?"

"Well, it's always nice to…"

"Oh, shut up," she snapped.

"May we come in?" asked Lloyd.

She stood there for the longest time holding the door and no doubt trying to make up her mind. "If you have to," she muttered, turned and disappeared into the darkness of the living room.

The two men cautiously stepped inside. The room was dark. There were no lights on, and even the windows were covered with black fabric along with the shades being drawn. They stopped just inside to give their eyes a chance to adjust.

"Kinda dark," said Lloyd.

"Yeah, well…just get used to it."

"May we sit down?" asked Lloyd.

"That's up to you," she said. "I really don't care one way or the other."

"Is the couch where it used to be?" asked Lloyd.

"In all the years you've known me, have you ever seen me move a thing in here?"

"What about the cats? I don't want to sit on one."

"They're out in the kitchen eating dinner. Besides, it wouldn't hurt to thin the herd by one or two."

The two men stumbled across the room and sat on the couch. As their eyes slowly adjusted to the dim light, they could finally make out the form of Belva sitting in her chair. She was holding onto what looked like a yardstick, and she was swatting it at something that was apparently flying around her head.

"Things haven't changed much around here," said Lloyd.

Belva began to rock her chair. She said nothing.

"Is your car running okay?" he asked.

"Yep," she said.

There was a long pause.

"Roof still leak over the kitchen?"

"Yep."

Another pause.

"Still got all of your cats?" asked Lloyd.

"Yep."

"How many?"

"Oh, I lost count. Damn things breed like rats."

"Why don't you get rid of them?"

"Don't think I haven't thought about that," she said swatting the yardstick in the air. "It puts a smile right on my face when I think about opening that front door and shooin' those God-awful buggers out of here."

At this point, Tony felt like he should try to jump into the conversation. "Why don't you?" he asked.

"What? Are you kidding?" she asked her voice loud and angry. "These cats are the only kin I got left. Everyone else either died on me or left me behind to fend for myself."

That last comment was quite a shot that she fired across Lloyd's bow. The air suddenly grew thick as everyone became silent. Here again, Tony thought it was a good time to break the ice, as it were.

"Can you remember your first cat?"

Belva smacked the floor with her yardstick. "Don't rightly remember."

Lloyd leaned forward. "It was Tom!"

"Huh?" asked Belva.

"Our first cat was named Tom."

Belva leaned back in her chair and smiled. "Yeah, you're right."

"He was the smartest cat I ever saw. Every morning, he would wake me up for school by slapping me in the face with his paw."

"I didn't know that," said Belva.

"The only bad thing is he didn't know how to read a calendar, so he would wake me on the weekends as well."

Belva chuckled aloud. "He was a smart one, that's for sure. When I'd put food in his bowl, he would scoot it into another room. Then he would return whining like he was hungry. I guess he figured he could con me out of another helping."

"I dearly loved that cat," said Lloyd.

"So did I," she said.

There was a long silence. Tony felt good about the reunion. Talking about cats was probably the only topic of conversation that gave them common ground.

"There's one thing I never understood about all that," said Lloyd. "If Tom was a male, how did we get stuck with a bunch of young ones?"

"The dumb ass got a female pregnant and then brought her home with him," she said. "I always thought that cat was a little weird. Before he knocked up that female, I thought for a while there that he was gay if there's such a thing as a gay cat."

Everyone laughed. Even Belva smiled and grunted.

"So, what are you two doing over here?" she asked. "You didn't come all the way over here to talk about my cats."

Lloyd's smile disappeared as he turned his stare to the floor. Tony could see it coming, so he jumped in ahead of Lloyd.

"Lloyd told me this thing had gone on long enough and that he missed you very much," said Tony.

A subtle smile appeared on Belva's face. "Is that right, Lloyd?"

"Yeah, what he said. I figured that you're my mother, and we shouldn't be mad at each other. After all, life is too short for stuff like this."

Belva grew silent. She began to rock her chair at a rapid pace then suddenly stopped. "I'm having meatloaf tonight," she announced.

"I'll be here," said Lloyd with a smile. He turned to Tony. "She makes the best meatloaf in the world."

Tony got to his feet. "No, thanks, I already have plans. He really didn't have any plans. It's just that he figured the two of them should be left alone to catch up.

"Come on," said Tony. "I have work to do."

Lloyd slowly got to his feet. He paused for a moment then walked across the room, leaned over and kissed his mother on the cheek. "See you later, Ma."

She wiped her eyes. "Don't forget. Meatloaf will be served at six."

"I'll be here," said Lloyd as he turned and walked out the door.

It was a long and quiet ride back to Lloyd's house. Lloyd smiled as he thought about what had just happened, and Tony felt a warm almost glowing feeling inside. He wasn't quite sure why he had it, but it felt good all the same.

He pulled into Lloyd's driveway and stopped the truck. Lloyd turned to Tony and thrust out his hand. "Thanks, my friend."

Tony took his hand. He felt the honest sincerity and appreciation in his firm handshake. "Don't mention it."

***

As Tony parked in front of the parsonage, he noticed a large black pick up truck that could only belong to Frank Bower. He walked upon the porch and peeked in the window. Sure enough, there was Frank sitting at the kitchen table with Wanda and Eddie. As Tony opened the door, Frank immediately got to his feet.

"Good morning, Mr. Franko," he said thrusting out his hand.

Now, here was Tony expecting the worst and finds Frank addressing him by his last name and waiting to shake his hand.

"Good morning, Mr. Bower," he said taking his hand.

"Call me Frank," he said.

"Okay…Frank."

"I'll bet you're surprised to see me," said Frank sipping his coffee. "Especially after our last encounter. By the way, please forgive me for such abusive and rude behavior. Trust me, it will never happen again."

"Sure…Frank," muttered Tony. He turned to Eddie to find him covering his mouth in an attempt to hide his laughter.

"I know what you're thinking," said Frank. "This is a bit strange for me to be acting like this, and I don't blame you for being a little shocked. Actually, I came over here for two reasons."

"And what might that be?" Tony asked.

"First of all, I want to thank you for what you did. You saved my grandson, and I'll never forget it."

Tony smiled. "Oh, that was nothing."

"Yes, it was something. You saved one of the most important people in my life."

"Anybody would have done the same."

"Doc Burns told me what you did. Not only did you carry Jimmy across town to the doc's office, you actually performed a miracle."

"I'm not so sure that it was…"

"The doc told me that Jimmy was dead," said Frank. "He was clinically dead, and you brought him back to life. He told me that you said a prayer for my grandson, and that brought him back to life. Is that right?"

"Well, yeah. I guess so."

"Well, Mr. Franko…"

"Call me Tony."

"If that is what you want…Tony. Like I said before, I came here for two reasons. The first reason was to thank you and tell you that no matter what you want, it's yours."

"Excuse me," said Tony with a puzzled look.

"You heard me," said Frank. "I feel a real need to pay you back for what you did. Anything you want is yours."

"Oh, no, Mr. Bower…"

Frank held up one finger and smiled. "Frank…remember?"

"I can't accept anything for what I did."

"Anything."

"That sounds tempting," said Tony.

"How about a new car? You'd look good driving a Corvette around town."

"Oh, good Lord."

"Anybody who saves the life of a Bower especially my grandson deserves to be rewarded," said Frank. "Now what will it be?"

There was a long pause. All eyes were focused on Tony.

"I got it," shouted Tony with his arms in the air.

"What do you want?" asked Frank.

"I want you to remove the dam that's blocking the creek, so that the water will flow again."

"I can't do that," said Frank.

"What do you mean?" said Tony. "You said anything."

"Anything but that."

"You are hurting those nice Amish families down the hill from you."

"I know," said Frank. "That's the whole idea."

"Why do you hate these people? Have they done something to you?"

"I really don't want to discuss them with you right now," said Frank. "I want to reward you for saving my grandson."

"The reward I want is for you to dismantle that dam."

"Sorry," said Frank.

Frustrated, Frank put his hands on his hips and stared at the floor. "What was the second reason you dropped by?"

"If you don't mind, I'd like to drive you over to the doc's office. Jimmy wants to see you."

"What does he want?"

"I don't know," said Frank. "He wouldn't tell me."

"Well, then, let's go."

It was a short ride to the doctor's office, and, yet, hardly a word was spoken. Tony was curious as to why Jimmy wanted to see him, but he was also reasonably certain that all he wanted to do was to personally thank him for saving his life.

Jimmy was in another room this time. They were keeping him for a couple days for observation. Frank and Tony stepped into the room and stopped at Jimmy's bedside. He opened his eyes and stared at the two men.

"Hi, Grandpa," he said.

"Jimmy, I want you to meet Mr. Franko," said Frank.

"Sure am glad to meet you, Mr. Franko," said Jimmy.

"Call me Tony."

"Sure thing...Tony."

"So, how are you feeling?" asked Tony.

"Fine."

"How soon are they going to let you out of here?"

"They said I might be able to go home tomorrow," said Jimmy.

"Well, that's fantastic," said Tony. "I'll bet you're ready to get out of here."

There was a pause.

"I wanted to thank you for what you did for me, Mr. Franko," said Jimmy. "That was a very altruistic thing you did."

Tony smiled and took a quick glance at Frank. "Wow! That's a pretty big word for a little boy like you."

"Jimmy, where did you hear that word?" asked Frank.

It was about that time that Jimmy's face grew solemn. His eyes were glazed over and he stared directly into Tony's eyes.

"You know, I passed away for a few minutes," said Jimmy.

"I know," said Tony. "I was there. In fact, I said a prayer for God to give you back your life."

"I know," said Jimmy. "I watched you."

"You watched me? How could you have watched..."

"I was told that I was returning to earth because of all the unfinished missions that were planned for me to carry out."

"Oh, is that right?" Tony asked as he smiled and gave a quick glance to Frank.

"One of those missions is to give you a message."

"Isn't that something?" said Tony with a voice that sounded slightly sarcastic. "And who is this message from?"

"Jesus Christ."

"Oh, for goodness sakes," said Tony with a smile and a playful voice. "You have a message to me from Jesus Christ and just what might that message be?"

Jimmy sat up in bed. "He said for you to let it go," said Jimmy.

"Let it go?"

"He said for you to let it go, and that Odell is safe with Him."

The playful smile disappeared from Tony's face. His mouth dropped open and he stared intently at the little boy lying in the bed in front of him.

"How did you know my brother's name?" asked Tony.

"Is your brother's name Odell?" asked Jimmy.

"Yes, it is. How did you know that?"

"I didn't."

Tony froze as his mind raced back and forth over what was said. He slowly straightened and turned to Frank. "Of course, he didn't. Nobody in this town knows my brother's name. You didn't, did you, Frank? You didn't know my brother's name, did you, Frank?"

"No, sir. Why? Where is your brother?"

Throughout history there have been special moments in certain peoples' lives. These people are called blessed, and the moment is called an epiphany. Tony's epiphany was like a lightening bolt from the heavens. It brought him to his knees and changed his life forever.

Frank stepped away from Tony who by now was on his knees and mumbling something half aloud. When he had finished, he got to his feet and slowly walked out of the room. For someone who wasn't aware of where he was or where he was going, it was a considerably long walk back to the parsonage. As he passed in front of the church, something happened to Tony. There was an unmistakable aching in his heart, an aching that he had not known since his brother died. It was that fateful day again, that day in the spring when two young boys made a fatal mistake that sent one to be with God and the other to his own, self-made hell.

Tony turned into the church. He opened the doors to the sanctuary and found the room empty and quiet. The only light in the room was sunlight filtered and seemingly glorified by the stain glass windows. The overwhelming colors fused with stray particles in the air creating halos of reds, greens, and blues. The intensity paled as it neared the floor producing colorful shadows that seemed to move with aimless purpose.

Tony was alone, and yet his heart was not. There was someone in the room. He could feel it. He could feel the strength of someone much stronger, much bolder, and much wiser than he. His heart was breaking now. Tears flowed down his cheeks and onto the floor. Tony fell to his knees and reached out to grab the robe of a God he had never really known until this very moment in time. He wept aloud with an intensity and hysteria that seemed to purge him of not only his grief but his earthly sins as well. He gripped the robe even tighter, and then as if God, Himself, was somehow entering into his body, Tony felt it. He felt the strength, a divine strength flow into his hands and then throughout his body. With this strength came a peace that only a few have ever known. It was a peace of mind and body that was never meant for mortals, and yet here was this young man bathing in a spiritual glow of divine peace.

"I feel your strength, God," said Tony. "I feel the peace wash over my body. It's a peace that neither I nor the likes of me have ever known. It gives me great comfort and joy knowing you. I give myself to you, my Lord. I will dedicate the rest of my life to the service of you and my fellow man. I know now the truth, the truth that few have witnessed. Please take my brother and keep him safe."

Tony released his hold and returned his hands to his sides. He bowed his head. "As I release my physical hold on you, the spirit of strength and peace remain inside. Thank you, dear God."

There was a stillness and a quiet like nothing Tony had ever known. The spirit was gone now, and yet it was still there. Tony could feel it deep inside him at his very core. The spiritual peace not only was within him, it was one with him. He could feel the strength of goodness within him and a knowledge of much grander things than he had even considered before. Yet, there was something missing. In spite of his new enlightenment, there was a very important unanswered question. In his heart, Tony knew God came to him with a purpose. God had an earthly mission for Tony, but he had no idea what it was. It didn't seem fair. God gave him the spiritual tools to do His work for a mission that was unclear. He would have to go on with his life. He would have to carry on and trust his own good judgment to recognize that which God would have him do.

The air was still now. The sanctuary had returned to a normalcy that Tony recognized. On the wall behind the podium was a large painting of Jesus knocking on a wooden door. Tony never could understand the meaning of that work of art. Surely the artist had something in mind. He must have designed it with a purpose or a message of some kind. Tony still wasn't quite sure what the artist wanted to say, but after today it had a very clear message to Tony. Jesus came knocking. He came knocking on Tony's door. Jesus has things for Tony to do, and, as far as Tony was concerned, He came knocking on the right door.

CHAPTER SIX

I turned to the bishop. Either he was not listening to me or was in shock. I wasn't quite sure. I leaned over and took his arm. "Are you okay?" I asked with a genuine concern.

"Yes," he said, batting his eyes as if awakening from a sleep. "I'm quite alright."

"I thought I lost you there," I said.

"In all my years, I've never heard a story quite like this one," said the bishop turning to Eddie. "Something tells me that this man was about to reap the benefits from this transformation of Tony."

"By all means, Tony was now the best assistant Eddie had ever mentored. In fact, there were times when Eddie wondered who was teaching whom. Not only was Tony doing what he was told, he was usually doing it long before Eddie had an idea that it needed to be done."

"After he had his epiphany, I would imagine Tony took his job a bit more seriously," said the bishop.

"Actually, Tony took just about everything more seriously," I said. "He was, indeed, a changed man, and the change was not just his attitude. He seemed driven, almost obsessed in a quest to help others. I don't know whether it was the fact that God gave him a mission that he could not identify, or he truly possessed the power of Jesus inside him. Either way, he made a profound impact on life as we knew here in this little town. He, himself, became a leader and a genuine inspiration to others."

"Every born leader has his critics," said Bishop Livingston. "How did Tony handle his?"

"Tony was great for reminding others of just how Jesus lived his life day after day. He devoted his life to helping people. There wasn't a selfish bone in the man's body. He was dedicated to the cause of helping others. Of course, we're mere humans and not expected to carry on day after day in the pursuit of easing the pain of others, however, Tony had a certain spin on that subject. He would point at his critics and ask them how much time out of each day are they following Christ's lead by helping other people. What have they personally done today for mankind? It's not possible to spend your whole life helping mankind. God never expected that, but He does expect you to feed a hungry person or give someone a ride. Tony usually got their attention when he pointed that finger of his and shouted, "What have you done today?"

There was a pause as the bishop shifted his weight in his chair. He smiled and turned once again to me. "I can't remember hearing such an intriguing story. I sense there is more to be told. It would seem that we started out talking about Father Rinehart, and now I'm not sure if this is a story of his life or that of Tony's."

"I understand your confusion," I said. "But one can't be told without the other. As I'm sure you can see their lives became intertwined and totally dependent on one another. What started out as a mismatch of the old and the new, of black and white, of two totally different cultures slowly evolved into a relationship between two men who loved God and each other."

"I have one more question that I need to know," said Livingston. "Did Tony ever figure out what his mission was?"

I grinned sheepishly at the bishop. "I can't tell you that, Bishop Livingston just yet. It would spoil the rest of my story."

"I understand," he said. "Then that tells me one thing."

"What's that?" I asked.

"Let's get on with the story."

"Well, let's see. Where were we? Ah, yes. Tony had just experienced his epiphany. That was a good place to stop considering we were now about to see the new and improved Tony. Don't get me wrong. Tony was still a human equipped with human frailties, weaknesses, likes and dislikes and the constant drive to have fun for; after all, there's only one God and only one perfect being. Tony was pretty serious in the beginning but soon succumbed to his human side and his forever quest to have fun. I think it was Eddie who convinced Tony that relaxing and having fun was God's idea. When He designed humans, I think He realized the need for such activity to counteract the serious side of life.

The next morning Eddie stumbled into the kitchen. To his surprise, Wanda was sitting at the table. She was drinking coffee and wearing a robe that not entirely covered her pajamas.

"What are you doing up?" asked Eddie.

"Couldn't sleep," she said.

"Does this mean you're making breakfast?"

"Nope."

"I had to ask," said Eddie. "By the way, where is Tony? I've looked everywhere for him."

"He's outside pulling weeds in the garden."

Now it was too bad there wasn't a camera nearby, so that somebody could have taken a picture of the shocked look on Eddie's face.

"And just why is he doing that?"

"How would I know," she said. "He's your playmate."

Eddie paused as he considered that last statement. He dearly wanted to address such a snide remark, but wanted much more to find out why Tony was pulling weeds. Eddie walked out of the house and started across the lawn. As he came near the garden, he could see Tony on all fours and routing through the tomato plants. Beside him was a pile of weeds.

"What in God's name are you doing, son?" he asked.

Tony rolled over into a sitting position. He rubbed the dirt from his hands. "Father Rinehart, since I've been here, I've pretty much been a pain in your backside, haven't I?"

Eddie stood there for a moment with a forced smile on his face. "Well, maybe in the beginning…"

Tony dusted off his knees as he got to his feet. "Let's face it. I've been more of a problem to you than an asset, and I plan to change that as of today."

Eddie stood there for a moment or two with a look of shock. "Let's go sit down on that bench over there."

The two men walked across the lawn and took a seat on a park bench under the shade of an oak tree. Eddie angled his body on the bench to face Tony. "Now, what's this all about? Something is wrong. I've never seen you quite like this."

Tony smiled. "Oh, far be it that something is wrong. On the contrary, in my whole life, I've never been so right."

"You seem so different," said Eddie. "You seemed to have matured almost overnight."

"Yes, in a way, I guess you're right. I have matured. I see things much differently now. From the streets of Detroit and right up until now, all I ever thought, felt, or did was for me. It has always been for me and everybody I have known a world of self-indulgence with no regard for even the closest people in our lives. It's all about me. That's how I have lived my life. That's how my family lived their lives. That's how my friends lived their lives.

It's all about me. What if we were to turn that around. What if it was all about you? What if we had a world that cared more about his neighbor than himself? Think of it, Father Rinehart. There would be no need for wars. There would be no more killings in the streets. No more senseless slayings in the name of some false God. We wouldn't have time for all that. We would be too busy taking care of others."

"So, what you're suggesting is that we follow in Christ's footsteps," said Eddie.

"What a wonder that would be," muttered Tony to nobody in particular. "When I was a kid, there was an old man who lived next door. It was hard for him to get around. Something was wrong with his legs. We never really knew what was wrong with them, but you could see when he was walking, he was in pain. As my friends and I grew older, of course, so did he. As he aged, his limp grew worse. You could see it in his face; his eyes actually winced with each step. Could you think of a better candidate for a neighbor who needed help? What did we do? We made fun of him when he would mow his lawn. The only mower he had was the old-fashioned type that had no motor. He was in so much pain, there were times I didn't think he would finish the lawn in spite of how small it was. We would actually mock his step in such a way that he could see us. We would say horrible things to him as well. Do you know what he did to us? Not a thing. Not one thing. He just kept on mowing his lawn.

Actually, when I think back on it, I really believe he was in too much pain to bother with the likes of us. The funny thing was he always treated me with respect. You know how it is when you're a kid. You pretty much get kicked around like a rented mule. But not Mr. Stoughton. He always treated me with respect almost as if I were an adult. My God, if only I could go back. I swear that man would never have had to mow his lawn again. How could I act like that? How could I treat a fellow human like that? How could God forgive me for such actions?"

Tony wiped his eyes as he turned to Eddie. "Since those days, I've asked God a million times to forgive me for the way I treated that kind old man. You've studied the Bible and know the ways of God. Is there any chance at all He has forgiven me?"

Eddie smiled a kind smile, a warm smile that, by itself, put Tony at rest and went a long way to ease his guilt. He slid his arm around Tony's shoulders. My son, it's not the mistakes you've made and the sins you've committed that define your life, it's what you do about them that really counts. We're all mere humans. We all make mistakes. The true sin is not learning from our transgressions and continue to repeat them throughout life. God forgave you the first time you asked Him for forgiveness. To Him it's forgotten, and He wants you to do the same. He wants you to learn from your mistakes and move on. God doesn't want you drowning in a sea of guilt. He has too many things in mind for you. He needs you at your best. Your atonement is to find an old man who is in pain and mow his lawn. Learn from the past, Tony, and move on to better things. God has a plan for you. He's got a lot of lawns for you to mow. The past, good or bad, is gone. It can't be changed. The future is yet to be. It could be years, months, or it could be tomorrow. Today is the day you plant seeds of goodness and prosperity. You're not going to change the world. God doesn't expect you to. He wants you to change your world and the lives of those within your world. Reach out, Tony. It's all right here in front of you. You've spent your life training and hoping to get into the game. Well, guess what? You're already in the game and don't know it. You're young with many years ahead of you. Don't wait any longer. Don't become an old man looking over his shoulder and wondering if he had done this or if he had done that. Don't be the one who drowns in a sea of regrets, broken promises, and lost relationships. Tony, you have a chance to step up to the plate with all the hope and promises that go with it. Don't miss that chance. I promise you that you will die burdened with regrets because you didn't do the right thing. Even if you don't hit a homerun, even if you strike out, guess what? You had your shot. You gave it your best. There's no curse that can befall you if you can honestly say that you did your best. It doesn't matter if you won. You gave it your best. That's all that matters, and that's all God expects."

By then, Tony was holding his head with both hands and occasionally wiping his eyes. "I wish I could have known you when I was growing up."

"What about your father? Wasn't he any help to you when you were a kid?"

"I never knew my father," said Tony. "Where I come from, fathers don't stick around. My mother was too busy working to raise us, so we were pretty much on our own. I guess we learned by trial and error."

"Under the circumstances," said Eddie. "I'd say you turned out pretty darn good. You're still a pain in the backside, but that's okay."

Tony smiled and took a deep breath. "Thanks Father, but I have to say I get this feeling that I was meant to do something important in my life. I just wish I knew what it was."

"The sad part is you may never know when it happens," said Eddie. "Here you are looking to change the world, and it maybe something as simple as your helping some young girl find her way or some young man who needs a friend or an ear to bend. You may not find a cure for cancer, but you might just help some young man develop a curve ball that gets him a professional baseball contract. So then you think what good was that? He's making a lot of money. How does that help others? Well, maybe he's the one who donates enough money to a cancer fund that leads to the cure. You just never know what God has up his sleeve if you pardon the expression. Actually, life is so simple, we don't get it. All we ever have to do is put our lives in God's hands. He's got it all worked for us, and since He wants the best for us, why not let Him do His thing?"

Tony turned and wrapped his arms around Eddie. In all my years, I don't think I ever experienced anything quite that touching. Here was a young black man from the city of Detroit teaming up with an older white man who just happened to be our priest. If ever there was a mismatch, and yet here we are just a short time later the two of them hugging each other.

"Thanks, Father," said Tony as he released his hold.

"What is it, my son?" asked Eddie. "You've changed so much. Don't get me wrong. I like what I see."

"Let's just say something happened to me," said Tony. "Something that changed my life forever."

"Care to tell me about it?"

"Maybe someday."

"It was about that time that the marshal showed up. Tony and Eddie looked up in time to see him walking across the lawn.

"Well, I'll be darned if it isn't Cooter Samples," said Eddie. "What are you doing out here, my friend?"

"I'm here on business," he said with a stone face. "I got that picture I said I would get of the escaped convict."

Eddie turned to Tony. "I always said that man was a credit to the police force here in these parts."

Cooter pulled a small wallet-sized photo from his pocket. "I'm afraid your new assistant here is a fraud," he said holding the photo in front of Eddie.

"Who's this?" asked Eddie studying the picture.

"This is your boy here."

Why do you say that?" asked Eddie. "That doesn't look anything like him."

"What are you talking about? He's a dead ringer."

"That's such a poor photo, Cooter. I think you've got the wrong man."

Cooter paused as he studied the photo. "You think so?"

"I know so," said Eddie. "Now get out of here with that and leave us alone."

Cooter was still looking at the picture. "What's your boy's name?"

Eddie paused. He glanced at Tony and then back to Cooter. "Jenkins...Keith Jenkins."

Cooter shrugged his shoulders and started across the lawn.

Tony watched as he disappeared and turned to Eddie. "You know, don't you?"

Eddie got to his feet. "Come on," he said looking away. "Let's go get some breakfast."

They were halfway across the lawn when Eddie turned to Tony. "We got to do something about that name of yours. Never did like it anyhow."

"Why's that?" asked Tony.

"Too Italian for the likes of you. We'll change it when we get you ordained. How would that be?"

"Sounds great," said Tony.

CHAPTER SEVEN

The diner was busy that morning. Most every seat was taken except for two that Earl Bass had saved. Eddie and Tony walked across the room and took a seat.

"It's about time," said Earl. "Nearly had to kill a few people to save your seats."

"Earl, you're a prince among men," said Eddie.

"Running a little late, aren't you, Ed?" asked Fred Munson.

Eddie smiled at Tony. "God keeps us hopping, Fred," he said.

Otis Hicks was halfway down the table. He leaned towards Eddie. "Enough of this crap," he said stretching even farther. "We were just talking about something you should be aware of."

There was a low murmur up and down the table.

"You can't go tellin' the Father here stuff like that," said Willard Barrow. "It just ain't fittin'."

"Go ahead," said Earl. "He ain't no priest anyhow…he's Eddie."

"Thanks for the shot to my ego," said Eddie. "Now what's the big problem?"

Otis glanced both ways then whispered, "Buford Hickman has been seen slipping in the back door of Mavis Red."

Everyone paused to see Eddie's reaction.

"Maybe Buford is stopping by for breakfast, or maybe he's doing some work for her. After all, that house of hers is about to fall down," said Eddie.

"Maybe he's stopping over there for some hanky panky," said Otis.

"Well, that's okay," said Eddie. "Mavis is single…has been single and probably will stay that way."

"Well, Buford isn't single," said Otis with a loud voice.

"Oh, for goodness sakes, Otis," said Eddie. "His divorce is final next week."

"We just don't think that it's right," said Otis.

"Good grief," said Eddie. "You old turds are worse than a couple of old women gossiping over the back fence. I think you're jealous that Mavis invited Buford over to her house and not you."

"You can think what you want," said Otis. "But what are you going to do about it?"

"What do you want me to do about it?"

"Go over there and talk to both of them."

"And tell them what?"

"That they are sinning, of course."

It was about that time that Clara Butts stopped at the table with an arm load of food. She set plates of food and cups of coffee in front of Eddie and Tony.

"Morning, Clara," said Eddie.

"Morning, Preach," she said picking up dirty dishes from the others.

"Has your boss ever considered serving anything else besides the same old eggs, bacon and toast?"

"Lloyd needs help picking out his white socks in the morning."

Eddie smiled. "And here I thought he was a business genius by serving only one meal."

"Frankly, that's the only thing he knows how to cook," she said.

Eddie lightly touched Clara's arm. "I know you're busy, but I have a question for you."

"Shoot."

"You keep up on the latest gossip around town," said Eddie. "Did you know that Buford Hickman has been seen visiting Mavis Red?"

"Yeah. So what?"

"Do you mind telling us what he's doing over there?"

"He's painting her kitchen the ugliest green I ever saw."

"You've been over there while he's at work?"

"Yeah, but that was a mistake."

"Why is that?"

"Because I had to look at that nasty looking green," said Clara. "Damn, that's one nasty color. Sorry about the damn, Preach."

"You beat everything, Otis," said Eddie sticking a fork in his eggs. "Now can I eat my breakfast?"

"Say, Eddie," said Fred Munson. "Did you ever raise enough money to put that elevator in the church?"

"We're still working on it," said Eddie sipping his coffee. "Why? Did you want to make up the difference?"

"Yeah, like that will happen," said Fred. "I can't even afford to pay attention."

"What's he talking about?" asked Tony wiping his mouth with a napkin.

"We're trying to raise enough money to put an elevator in the church," said Eddie. "It's going to cost nearly as much as it did to build the church in the first place."

"Why do we need an elevator?" asked Tony.

"Well, there are those who can't walk up the steps."

"Like who?"

"Well, there's Ethyl Carter," said Eddie. "She's getting along in years and has trouble."

"So, how does she get in the church?"

"Somebody helps her."

"That's funny. She climbed the stairs last Sunday with no help."

"Then there's Skip Bigalow," said Eddie. "He's in a wheelchair."

"Which one is Skip Bigalow? I don't believe I've seen anybody in a wheelchair."

"He hasn't been to church in over two years."

"Let me guess," said Tony. "Somebody helped him up the steps as well."

Eddie sipped his coffee. "Why the concern for our elevator? It's obvious that you are not in favor of it."

Tony finished his last bite and wiped his mouth. "I've made so many mistakes in my life that I finally decided to change the direction of my decision making. I decided that whenever I have an important decision to make, I'm going to ask myself which direction would Jesus want me to go."

"What's that got to do with our elevator?"

"I don't think Jesus would want you to do that."

"You can't be serious," said Eddie.

"Oh, I'm dead serious."

Eddie took a deep breath. "Okay, so why wouldn't Jesus approve?"

"I think that money could be used for more humanitarian purposes. Our church provides spiritual help for a lot of the residents in this town. Unfortunately, there are people in this town who need more than that. There are those who are in trouble and need our financial support as well."

"Our church does its part to help others," said Eddie.

"I'm not denying that," said Tony. "But our part would be considerably bigger if we had the thousands of dollars you're about to spend on an elevator."

"Well, I suppose we..."

"Let me ask you a question," said Tony. "If Jesus were the in charge, do you think He would spend the money on an elevator so that Mr. Bigalow once a year could enter the church without help, or would He be more concerned about Clarence Jones who lost his job and is having trouble feeding his family?"

Eddie turned to Tony with an exasperated look. "I don't know what happened to you, but I'm not all sure I like it."

"Tony smiled. "Just thinking out loud."

"Hey, Eddie," shouted Otis from the other end of the table. "I hear Cooter is looking for an escaped convict. He just happens to be black, and he escaped right around the time your assistant over there showed up."

All of a sudden that table full of gossiping old timers went quiet. Everyone knew that what Otis had just said was not only bold but borderline accusative.

"Is that right?" asked Eddie.

"You don't know whether he caught that desperate escapee from the prison, do you?" asked Otis.

"Can't say as I have," said Eddie.

"Tony leaned over. "Let me at him," he whispered to Eddie.

Eddie grabbed Tony by the arm. "No, let me handle this." He turned to Otis. "If I were you, Otis Hicks, I'd be expecting a visit from Cooter yourself."

"Why is that?" asked Otis with a smirk.

"Somebody stole a bunch of chickens from Lester Skaggs the other night."

"Well, what's that got to do with me?"

"I'd say you're the perfect suspect."

The smirk disappeared from Otis' face. "And why is that?"

"You're white, aren't you?"

"Yeah, so what?"

"Lester got a glimpse of the man who stole his chickens, and he was white," said Eddie with a loud enough voice so that everyone in the restaurant could hear him. "That makes you a suspect."

The room erupted in snickers and quiet laughter.

"You know if you weren't a priest..." said Otis.

"Ed, I do have some good news for you," said Fred Munson.

"What is it, Fred?" Eddie asked. "I could use it."

"Peggy Sue is back in town."

Eddie froze. He looked at Fred. "Peggy Sue Nichols?"

"The one and only Peggy Sue I'd-Do-It-For-Nickels."

"Wonder what she's doing in town."

"I heard she came here to see you," said Fred."

The table erupted in childish cat-calls and laughter.

Eddie drained his coffee and got to his feet. "Come on, Tony," he said starting for the door. "Let's get out of here."

Tony paused as he stared at the man storming out of the diner. He had seen him upset before but nothing like this. "What about the bill?" he asked holding up a piece of paper.

Eddie opened the door with one hand and pointed at the table with his other. "Let them pay it. They never go to church, so they can write it off as a donation."

By the time Tony dropped some money on the table and got outside, he had to jog just to catch up with Eddie. He tried to match Eddie's stride but found himself still jogging to keep up.

"So, are you going to tell me who Peggy Sue is?" asked Tony.

"It's none of your business, and her name isn't Peggy. It's Margaret."

"Then why did everyone call her Peggy?"

"Peggy is another name for Margaret."

"What?"

"Peggy is like a nickname for Margaret."

"When did that happen?"

"It's always been like that," said Eddie. "Everybody knows that. It's like Jack and John."

"What about Jack and John?"

"Never mind," said Eddie. "Besides, it's none of your business."

"She broke your heart, didn't she?"

"You can't just let it go, can you?" asked Eddie.

"I'm concerned for you," said Tony. "You're obviously upset."

"I'm not upset. I just don't want to talk about Margaret, so put a lid on it."

The rest of the trip back home was a bit tense. At first, Tony joked and kidded Eddie about his past love. He had no intentions of upsetting Eddie over this matter, but he had no idea how serious it was to him. When they got back to the parsonage, Eddie said that he had work to do in the church and told Tony not to bother him.

Eddie spent the next two hours doing busy work in the sanctuary. He couldn't quite understand it, but in his heart he knew that Margaret would soon be coming to visit him. That, in itself, stirred a range of emotions for Eddie that left him in a state of total confusion. She was the only one he had ever loved. Oh, there had been others. Eddie dated girls as a teenager just like everybody else did, but Margaret was different. She was the one. He tried not to fall in love with her, but he couldn't help himself. He even tried staying away from her but soon found it to be impossible. Then when she discovered that Eddie would soon be going to school to become a priest, she broke off their relationship. Eddie's world collapsed around him. He knew it was the right thing, but that didn't make it any easier. He never really was quite the same, and even after all the years he was still in love with her.

Eddie was bent over polishing the wood on one of the pews, when he heard the front door open. He could feel his heart pounding in his chest. He stood and turned. There she was, even more beautiful than he remembered. She was tall and thin, dressed in business attire.

Eddie had an uncommonly broad smile. "Good morning, Margaret."

"Ah, yes," she said. "I'd almost forgotten. One of the reasons I've always loved you is because you always called me Margaret. I never could get used to Peggy. How are you, Eddie, or should I call you Father Rinehart?"

Eddie lifted his hand. "Eddie sounds just fine."

Margaret walked slowly down the aisle as she scanned the interior of the sanctuary. "Beautiful church," she said aloud.

"Thank you," said Eddie. "We're proud of her."

"How have you been?" she asked.

"Oh, I can't complain," he said, his voice slightly quivering.

Margaret stopped in front of him and pointed at the pew. "May I?"

"By all means," he said and sat down next to her.

There was a long pause. Margaret fondled her earring while Eddie's foot bounced up and down.

"Have you seen many of our old classmates?" asked Eddie.

"Not since our last reunion."

"You heard that John Miller died?"

"Yes, I did hear something about that," she said.

Another long pause.

"So, tell me," said Eddie. "Did you end up marrying Frankie?"

She turned to Eddie with a surprised look. "Frankie?"

"Frank Rivers...the guy you dated after...me," said Eddie with a sheepish grin.

"Oh, that Frankie," she said. "No, Frankie was not really my type. In fact, I can't imagine any woman who would consider him any type at all. No, I never married. Oh, I guess you might say I got married. Actually, I married my job."

"What do you do?"

"I'm an advertising consultant," she said sitting straight in her seat. "I love my job, but it does keep me on the move. Can't remember the last time I spent a whole week at home."

"That's really great," said Eddie. "Not many people these days can say they love their jobs."

"What about you?" she asked. "How do you like being a priest?"

"Well, the job is a challenge, sometimes overwhelming, but, yeah, I love it. My boss can sometimes be tough," he said with a smile.

"It was years after we graduated before I heard about it," she said. "Let me tell you what a shock that was. I mean after all the dates we had."

Eddie blushed. "Oh, I wasn't that bad."

Margaret pointed her finger at Eddie. "Well, that's your story, mister. The way I remember it, you had six hands."

Eddie laughed. "Those were good days, weren't they?"

"Yes, they were," she said with a warm smile. "I often look back on them. Actually, I've thought about you quite often over the years."

"I've thought about you as well...even if you did break my heart when you broke it off."

"I broke it off?"

"Yes, you broke it off, and I can prove it," said Eddie. "I still have the Dear John letter that you gave me."

"Well...I guess I'm busted," she said with a grin. "You saved that letter after all these years?"

"I still have the tickets to the prom, movie ticket stubs from our dates and every picture I ever took of you."

"Wow!" she said. "It would almost seem as if you still have a thing for me."

"Thing for you?" he asked. "You could say I still have a thing for you."

"Ever wonder what might have been?" she asked.

"Do you mean you and me?"

"Yeah. Ever wonder what kind of life we would have had together?"

"Most everyday."

Margaret's smile became a slight grin, and her stare turned to the floor. "Kinda sad, isn't it?"

"Very much so," said Eddie. "I think we would have made a great team."

"Eddie, may I ask you a very personal question?" she asked shifting her weight.

"Sure, go ahead."

"As I understand it, when you're a priest, you can't get married. Is that correct?"

"That's correct."

"Have you ever had any regrets?" she asked. "I mean, you knew this when you signed on, didn't you?"

"Yes, I was aware of the rules, but I was young, stubborn and thought I knew everything. Don't get me wrong, I love being a priest. I love helping people and serving God. There's much satisfaction in the job. Just last week, I was counseling a young couple who were in the process of getting a divorce. After two months of working with these two, they are going to give it another try. They might not make it, but it sure validates my life when I get a victory like this."

"What are your regrets?"

"What are my regrets?" stated Eddie as if it were a statement rather than a question. "Every time I see a young mother and father walk in here with their children reminds me that I'm going home tonight to an empty house. That's a regret. Every time I go to the theater and sit behind two young people holding each other and stealing a kiss or two is a regret. When it seems that everyone in the world has someone to hold and to love, and I have nobody. That not only is a regret but a deep hurt as well. I know that I chose this life. It's my love for Christ that guides my life, but it doesn't change anything. I still hurt inside. I still want what everyone else has and usually takes for granted. I watched life go by wondering what it would have been like. Wondering if she would have been as pretty and smart as you. Wondering if she would have been as easy going as you. Wondering still if she would have been you. Still, all-in-all, I sometimes wonder if I hadn't become a priest, would I have lived to regret that? I guess it all comes down to following what your heart tells you and become the best priest or husband that you can possibly be."

"Do you ever feel resentment to the church for your loneliness?" she asked wiping her eyes.

"Good heavens, no," he replied. "It was ultimately my decision, and, let's face it, God has me right where He wants me."

"To tell you the truth, when you started dating Marie after we broke up, I thought for sure you would marry her."

"She was a wonderful girl," he said taking a deep sigh.

"You miss her, don't you?"

Eddie smacked his legs with both hands. "So, tell me about yourself. We've wallowed in my sordid past long enough."

Margaret forced a grin. "Well, my past isn't much better. If it weren't for my work, I don't know what I would do."

"Any boyfriends along the way?"

"A few...nothing serious."

Eddie's eyes lit up and his face became a smile. "Ever wonder if you and I were meant to be?"

"What do you mean?"

"Maybe down deep, we both believe that we were meant to be together. We might not even be aware of it, but it's there guiding our lives. Ever wonder why you came back home? To be more specific, why did you stop in to see me?"

She paused. "I don't know," she said with a puzzled look. "I know I wanted to see you again."

"I'm telling you," said Eddie. "That's God at work trying to bring us back together."

"I suppose it's possible, but..."

"I love you, Margaret," said Eddie. "I always have and always will."

"Eddie, I'm so flattered, but you can't...we can't..."

"Why not? Why can't we be happy? Why do we have to be lonely?"

"But I'm not lonely, Eddie."

Eddie paused. "What do you mean?"

"I'm not lonely. Like I told you before, I married my job. When I said that, I meant it."

Eddie forced a frantic smile. "I hate to tell you this, but it has been known to have a job and be married as well."

"I know it's hard to understand," she said. "But I love my job so much there is no room in my life for a husband or even a boyfriend. Too many years have gone by. Yes, Eddie, I love you. Even when we broke up all those years ago, I never stopped loving you, but it's just too late. There's no going back."

Eddie reached for her hand and held it with both of his hands. "You know what I'm telling you? I'm willing to give up my job which is the love of Christ. I'm willing to give it all up for you."

Margaret gave him a warm and sympathetic smile. "I'm sorry, Eddie."

Eddie tightened his grip on her hand as if he never wanted to let go, and yet his voice was now more subdued with less resolve. "Seems funny. This journey that we call life takes us for quite a ride. There are twists and bends, blind alleys and wrong turns. God gives, and He takes. There are good times and bad. We come across so much beauty in this life and yet so much unspeakable ugliness of all kinds. We all wonder if we made the right choices...took the right fork in the road. We convince ourselves that we can always do it all over or change our lives if it doesn't work out, but there is always that one problem. That problem lurks in the shadows like a predator. That unseen and unforgiving monster is time. Our lifetime here on earth is only a brief moment in the universe, and yet we blatantly and, yes, even arrogantly choose to ignore it. The days, months and years fly by without notice or even concern, until one day we look in the mirror and discover a stranger glaring back at us. By then, we know in our hearts that it's too late. The monster won. It was a patient killer always stalking you, never giving up. It is relentless and untiring, waiting to, in the end, consume your very being. I'm amazed at how many people think they can avoid even escape the monster's pursuit. It seems harmless enough. Just a ticking clock on the wall. But it's got you in its sights. And here I am wishing I could stop that clock, yea, even turn back the hands to give me one more chance." Eddie paused and turned an empty stare to the floor. "Give me one more chance to hold a baby in my arms and know he is of my blood. Give me one more chance to look lovingly into the eyes of the woman who gave him to me and give thanks to the one who blessed me with this miracle."

Margaret pulled her hand away from his and wrapped her arm around his shoulders. "I'm sorry," she said softly.

Eddie wiped his eyes. "Shame on me," he said his voice more upbeat. "Here you take the time to come over here to see me, and I end up like this."

"Don't say that," she said. "I'm proud that you confided in me."

Eddie turned to her and took both of her hands. He forced a big smile and said, "If you ever change your mind, I'll be here. You know how I feel."

Tears streaked down her cheeks. "Yes, I know how you feel," she said getting to her feet. "And who knows?

I've been thinking about retirement and moving back home."

Eddie wrapped his arms around her. "Take care, my friend."

"Take care of yourself," she said breaking away. "I'll see you again real soon." With that, she turned and walked out of the room.

CHAPTER EIGHT

As Tony opened the back door of the parsonage, he found Wanda with a cup of coffee sitting at the kitchen table.

"Do you ever work around here?" he asked taking a seat.

"I do more work accidentally than you do on purpose," she snapped.

"Excuse me," he said. "I know you've got this coffee drinking thing down pretty good but was wondering if that's all you do around here."

Wanda paused then smiled. "Is there something wrong? You seem a bit irritated unlike your normal self."

Tony ran his hand through his hair. "I'm sorry, but I'm worried about Father Rinehart."

Wanda smiled. "You needn't trouble yourself about him right now. He's going to come through this just fine."

Tony turned to her his face expressionless. "He's going to come through what?"

"These feelings he has harbored all these years for Margaret are going to finally be exposed. It will do him good to get them out on the table."

"How do you know about Margaret?"

"Oh, my goodness, boy. Wanda knows everything," she said with a big smile.

"Yeah, but you haven't had a chance to talk to Father Rinehart since he learned that she was back home."

Wanda paused, her face grew solemn. "It isn't Father Rinehart that worries you, is it?"

"What do you mean?"

"Something is troubling you," she said. "You have these new feelings that you don't understand. What is it, Son? What is it that bothers you?"

Tony stared at her for a moment. "Somehow I get the feeling you already know the answer before I do."

"No, no," she said. "Just tell me what's on your mind."

Tony scratched his head and grimaced. "I get this feeling that I have something important that God wants me to do. Actually, it's kinda funny. A short time ago, I didn't even believe in God, and now I consider Him a close friend."

"God has a plan for you," she said with an air of confidence. "He has a mission that He wants you to fulfill."

"For some reason, I believe you."

"There are those who need our help, and we can't turn our backs on them," she said. "Our churches are encumbered with too many rules, too many do's and do nots. There is an obligation to sing hymns, pray and take communion, and that's about where it ends. We go back to our daily lives the next week and hope that the priest forgives our sins next Sunday when we sing hymns, pray and take communion all over again."

"I don't understand," said Tony. "Isn't that the function of a church?"

Wanda leaned forward. "If Jesus was a pastor or a priest, how do you think He would use the church? It's just my opinion, but I believe the church of Jesus Christ would be a Mecca for the homeless, a haven for sinners and a place of nourishment for the hungry. Jesus isn't just worried about you and me. He loves, cares for us and tries to guide us as we walk the journey of life, but there are many who are less fortunate and need His help. You may have heard the old expression: His eye is on the sparrow. He not only looks out for the lowly sparrow but the man who lost his job, his house and family, and is now holding a gun up to his head. He worries about the woman who has nothing left in her house to feed her children or the child whose parents are getting a divorce. Yes, He has his eye on the sparrow and a whole lot more, and those who believe in Him will grow above and beyond their own problems and will soon have their eyes on the sparrow as they learn to serve God and their fellow man. You see, to God we are all angels right here on earth. Somebody right this minute is praying to God for an angel to watch over them and help them with their problems. Once you change your life and begin to walk in Jesus' footsteps, you will open your eyes and your heart to do what you can to help that somebody. In other words, you will become that somebody's angel. Do you see what I'm trying to tell you? Jesus wants you to become one of His angels."

Wanda leaned back in her chair and sipped her coffee.

"I want to help, but I don't know what He wants me to do," said Tony.

"You've already begun and don't even know it."

"What do you mean?"

"Didn't you reunite Belva with her son?"

Tony smirked. "But that wasn't anything great."

Wanda held up a finger. "Eye on the sparrow," she said with a knowing smile. "Didn't you save little Jimmy's life?"

"Well, yes, I suppose…"

"You were Jimmy's angel and didn't even realize it," she said leaning forward once again. "Your time is coming, my son. God has a mission for you, and it's coming soon."

"How will I know what it is?"

"You'll know."

"What do you mean by that?"

Wanda got to her feet. "Break is over," she said. "I've got work to do. Why don't you go over to the church and check on your buddy?" She then turned and disappeared out of the kitchen.

Tony sat there for a moment or two thinking about what had been said, then got to his feet and walked out the door. He started for the front door that led to the sanctuary but changed his mind. Eddie had said he was going to be working there, so Tony decided to enter the church through the back door. As he opened the door and closed it behind him, he heard a noise coming from the kitchen. He turned just in time to see the door on the refrigerator close.

"Who's there?" he called out. "He then heard the scuffling of shoes as if someone was running, and, yet, there was no one visible. He rushed across the room and opened the door to the kitchen. Just as he did, a young boy who was bent over ran near him. He reached out and grabbed him. The boy struggled, but Tony had a firm grip.

"Who are you?" asked Tony.

"That's none of your business," said the boy.

"Nobody is going to hurt you," said Tony. "This is a church. We don't normally beat up little boys."

"Then, why don't you let me go?"

"I will if you tell me your name."

The boy stopped struggling. "Bryan...Bryan Gibbs."

Tony slowly released his grip. "What were you doing in here?"

"It's still none of your business."

"Bryan...you were messing around in my church without permission. Yes, it is my business. Now, what were you doing?"

Bryan paused; his frightened stare turned to the floor. "I was trying to find something to eat."

"Why?" asked Tony. "Don't you have anything to eat at home?"

"No."

"How many are in your family?"

"Just my mom and my little sister."

"Where is your Dad?"

"I don't know," said Bryan. "I never knew him."

"Does your mother work?"

"She used to, but she was in a car accident and lost one of her legs."

"So, you were not only getting something for you to eat, but you were going to take some food back home. Is that right?"

"I have a dollar to pay for some food.

"Where do you live?" Tony asked.

Bryan pointed. "Over there."

"How far over there?"

"Two blocks."

Tony stared at the boy for several moments. "Do you mean to tell me that you and your family live only two blocks from this church, and the three of you are starving?"

The young boy simply nodded his head.

"That's disgraceful," Tony muttered. He turned and started for the refrigerator. "Come with me." With giant steps, Tony walked across the floor to the refrigerator and opened it up. There were hamburgers, hotdogs and buns leftover from last weekend's cookout. He grabbed a grocery bag, loaded it with everything left behind and handed it to Bryan. "Here, take this home with you." Bryan took the bag and started for the door. Tony pointed at the boy. "You come back here in two days, and I'll have more food for you."

Tony stormed out of the kitchen and into the sanctuary. Eddie was sitting in the front row of pews with his head bowed. Tony hesitated for a moment then marched on down to the front of the room.

"Did you know that there are starving women and children, and they live only two blocks from this church?" asked Tony emphatically.

Eddie shook his head as if he were coming out of deep thought. "What did you say?"

Tony sat down beside him. "There are people who live just two blocks from our church, and they have nothing to eat. We're talking about little kids going to bed with empty stomachs."

"Well, I'm sorry to hear that, but what's that got to do with me?" said Eddie.

Tony leaned forward. "I don't believe what I'm hearing. Our neighbors are starving, Eddie. Shouldn't we do something about that?"

Eddie eased back in the pew. "There are government agencies that take care of things like that."

"Government agencies? Wouldn't you say they've kinda dropped the ball? I just caught a kid stealing food from our refrigerator."

"I hope you called Cooter on him," said Eddie.

"Good Lord, Eddie!" said Tony. "The kid and his family are starving!"

"Well, what did you do?"

"I gave him everything we had in the kitchen," said Tony. "If I had thought of it, I would have taken him over to your place and cleaned out your pantry."

"Well, that seems a bit extreme."

"A bit extreme? What's happened to you? How could you take this subject so lightly?"

"I'm not taking this lightly," said Eddie. "It's just that there's nothing I can do."

Tony paused then pointed at Eddie. "Now, I get it. Now, I know why you have no passion for this problem...this most basic need of humans. You've never been hungry. Oh, I'm not talking about the hunger pangs between meals. I'm talking about how you feel after days of not eating, what it feels like to pass out from lack of food. I've been there, Mister, and it ain't no fun. You know after so long, you start to develop sores. I don't know why, but I've seen them and I've had them. Then when you finally find a piece of meat in a garbage can and you brush off the maggots before you devour it, you know you're going to get sick, but you just don't care."

"I'm sorry, Tony," said Eddie. "And you're right. I don't know what it's like to be hungry, but what can we do about it?"

"I'll tell you what we can do about it. We can open a kitchen or whatever you call it. Even if it's only once a week, at least that's one good meal some of these people might get."

"Are you serious?" asked Eddie.

"Why not? We've got that huge kitchen down there with everything we would need just going to waste."

"Where are you going to get the food?" asked Eddie. "And who's going to do all the work?"

"These are all minor details," said Tony. "We'll work them out."

Eddie ran his hands through his hair. "I don't know. The church has never done anything like this."

"Don't you think it's about time?"

"The bishop will never allow it."

"Then we won't tell him."

"I don't know, Tony," said Eddie. "I've never done anything like this."

"Let me ask you a question," said Tony moving even closer. "If Jesus was our bishop, what do you think He would say?"

Eddie smiled, shook his head and gazed out the window. "You really are into this, aren't you?"

Tony took one of Eddie's hands and covered it with both of his hands. He then looked him in the eyes and said, "Last night, I said a prayer. It was only the second prayer in my life, but seeing as how the first one worked so well, I thought I would try it again."

"Well, what did you say?" asked Eddie.

"I said, 'Lord, don't let me remain where I am. Help me reach where You want me to be."

Eddie paused, then he smothered Tony's hands with his. "Go for it," he said with a smile.

"Thank you, sir," said Tony.

"Sir? That's a first."

"Don't expect it too often."

"Just remember," said Eddie pointing his finger. "If the bishop finds out, we're all done."

"Got 'cha."

"It will have to done without any financial help from the church."

"Not a problem."

Eddie slowly shook his head. "Whatever happened to that smart-ass kid from Detroit?"

Tony smiled. "I guess he found out what life is all about."

CHAPTER NINE

The next morning brought low lying rain clouds that seemed to touch the ground. Tony opened the front door of the café, and Eddie and he walked inside. As usual there was a lively discussion at the center table. In fact, it was so lively, hardly anyone noticed their arrival. Half of them were talking about the Viet Nam War, and what they would do if they were in charge. The other half was discussing politics, namely President Johnson and what he should do to end the war.

"Lively bunch this morning," said Eddie.

"Yeah. They're all riled up," said Tony. "I've never seen them this crazy."

"They get that way when they talk politics."

Clara Butts was nearly running as she sped by the table. She dropped off coffee and water for both Eddie and Tony without stopping.

"You gotta love a small town," said Tony

"Why is that?"

"Where else can you sit down in a public place, and a woman brings you your breakfast, and you don't even have to ask for it?"

Fred Munson leaned forward. "I hear Peggy stopped by to see you. How did it go?"

The room became silent.

Eddie had a disgruntled look on his face. "Fred, can you tell me the last time a woman even kissed you on the lips?"

Fred sat back. "That's kinda personal, isn't it?"

"My point exactly," said Eddie. "Some things are personal, and Peggy or Margaret is my personal thing. Now let's just forget about it."

"Aw, come on," said Otis Hicks. "That can only mean that you struck out with her."

"Hey, Otis," said Tony. "I hear you've been seeing Cecil Green's wife. Is that true?"

Otis bristled. "Certainly not."

"Well, that's what I heard," said Tony. "And it was from someone right here in this room."

Otis slowly scanned the table of men. "Alright...which one of you yahoos was it?"

"He's pullin' your chain, Otis," said Willard Barrow. "He turned the spotlight from Eddie onto you. The kid is good."

Clara swung by the table and dropped plates of food in front of Tony and Eddie.

"I'm starved," said Eddie picking up a fork. He turned and looked at Tony who was obviously lost in thought. "Are you alright?"

Tony smiled and held up a finger. "I've got it," he said to no one in particular. "The answer was right here in front of me, and I didn't see it."

Eddie frowned. "What answer to which question? What are you talking about?"

Tony got to his feet. He then tapped on his water glass with a fork.

"Good Lord," said Eddie. "Now what?"

"Gentlemen, may I have your attention?" Tony announced.

The room became silent except for Cletus Trimble. "This better be good," he said. "My coffee is cold, Earl just sneezed on me and now I have to listen to a speech."

Tony cleared his throat as if to tell Cletus to shut up. "We have a problem," he said in a loud voice. "We have a problem right here in LaRue."

"I'll say we have a problem," said Cletus. "Willard over here just pinched off an air biscuit, and good Lord does it ever smell."

Tony was forced to speak even louder to drown out the laughter. "The problem we have is that there are people starving in this town."

Cletus held up a finger to get Tony's attention. "You tell any starvin' people to help themselves to any beans left in Willard's pantry just so he don't hurt nobody."

Tony ignored Cletus and continued, "I don't think you understand how serious…"

Then Otis held up his hand to something. "Now if you ask me…"

Just then, Eddie did something that had never been done before and was talked about for years. He stood and, at the top of his voice, announced, "Shut the hell up! Tony has something important to tell you, and I want you to listen to him!" Every man, woman, and child in that restaurant froze. There was complete silence throughout the room. People who were chewing their food stopped. There was even one man who was carrying a forkful of food to his mouth, and it froze as if he had been posing for a picture.

Tony cleared his throat and began again. "What I want to do is to provide a free dinner on Saturday nights for anyone who needs it," said Tony with a shaky voice.

"Good Lord," said Otis. "There are people all over this county who are out of work. My guess is you are looking at a hundred or so standing in line. Just for shits and giggles, who's going to cook for all these starving people?"

Tony scratched his head. "I'm not quite sure."

Cletus held up his hand and began to speak at the same time. "Where are you going to get the food and supplies?"

"I don't know," said Tony.

"You're going to need a bunch of people to pull this off," said Earl. "Who are you going to get to help you?"

"Well, I was kinda figuring on all of you guys," said Tony his eyes searching for a reaction.

All of the men at the table exchanged glances and then laughed hysterically. Tony was stunned with humiliation. He dropped back down in his seat with his eyes staring at the wall.

Eddie grabbed Tony by the arm and got to his feet. "Come on," he said. "Let's get out of here."

***

It was early evening. The setting sun poured through the colored-stained windows casting eerie shadows throughout the sanctuary. Earlier, Tony had slipped out of the parsonage and found in the backroom of the church two bottles of wine that were used for communion. It was now two hours later. One bottle was empty lying on its side on the floor. Tony had a grip on the neck of the second one which was by now nearly empty.

Eddie walked into the sanctuary. He paused when he saw Tony slouched in the pew, his head held back and passed out.

"Tony….are you okay?" asked Eddie.

Tony's eyes opened as slits. "Huh?"

"Are you okay?"

Tony slowly sat straight. "Yeah…I'm okay."

Eddie smiled and lightly kicked the empty bottle on the floor. "You know, we don't normally serve this much wine at communion."

Tony said nothing.

"Of course, it might not be such a bad idea," said Eddie. "Might loosen them up a little."

Eddie sat next to Tony and looked him in the eyes. The smile disappeared from Eddie's face. Something was wrong. It wasn't just the wine either. He had peered into eyes like this before, eyes that hid deep sorrow and anguish. He knew that Tony was upset over the experience at the diner, but there was something more.

"Are you alright, Tony?"

Tony turned to Eddie, his eyes wandering, trying to focus. "I, the Lord of wind and flame, I will tend the poor and lame," recited Tony his voice slurring the words.

Eddie smiled. "That's HERE I AM, LORD. We sang that last Sunday."

Tony turned away from Eddie. "I will set a feast for them. My hand will save. Finest bread I will provide till their hearts be satisfied. I will give my life to them."

Eddie placed his hand on Tony's shoulder. "I'll bet you're still upset about this morning. Well, don't give it another thought. I'll get those rednecks to help you with your kitchen. Most of those idiots owe me big time, and they're about to pay me back."

Tony showed no reaction. He sat there motionless, and soon a tear fell down his cheek. "I the Lord of sea and sky, I have heard my people cry. All who dwell in dark and sin my hand will save. I, who made the stars of night, I will make their darkness bright."

Eddie pulled him close in a one-arm hug. "What's wrong, my son? Something is troubling you."

Tony shook himself free of Eddie's grasp and slid across the pew. "Why do bad things have to happen?"

"Something bad happened to you?"

"Bad things happen to everybody," said Tony his eyes finally opening wide. "A bridge collapses killing people, wars kill millions, even…even a young boy robbing a store with his brother gets gunned down in the street and dies in his brother's arms."

Eddie paused. "He was your brother, wasn't he?"

Tony held up his hands and stared at the fading light filtering through the windows. "I do believe in God, but I just don't understand why He allows bad things to happen to us."

Eddie thought for a moment. He knew this issue was the root of Tony's sorrow, and he also knew how important his answer could be.

"You know, Tony, when I was a young man studying to be a priest, I ran across this little religious cartoon. I began to read it thinking it was supposed to be funny. After all, religious people have a sense of humor. In fact, I've always hoped that God had one as well, so that He would laugh at some of the dumb things I've done in my life. Anyhow, in the first panel of the cartoon were three men carrying a cross that was very large not unlike the cross that Jesus bore. You could tell that the three men were struggling to carry such a weight. It was so large that it dragged on the ground well behind them. The second panel of the cartoon had one on the men turned to the heavens and tell God that the cross was too heavy and would He cut part of it off. The next panel shows the same three men carrying crosses except the one man's cross is now a bit shorter than the others. His burden is lighter, but it's still too heavy. He turns to heaven again and tells God that it's still too heavy and would He shorten it again. The next panel shows the three men approaching a great chasm or a gorge if you like. Two of the men dropped their crosses and they connected to the other side creating a bridge for them to cross over, while the third man could not. By asking God to shorten his cross and ease his burden, he was unable to cope with the adversity that lay in front of him. Tony, life throws burdens and adversities at us all the time. They make us strong to take on the real challenges that we face. There are easy way outs all along life's journey. The true test is how we resolve these challenges. Do we take that easy way out, or do we confront them head on?"

Tony looked into Eddie's eyes. Tears were gushing down his face. It was clear that the sorrow he had buried all these years was now within his grasp.

Eddie took Tony's hand. "Your brother's death is eating you alive, isn't it?"

"He didn't even want to be there," said Tony weeping aloud. "He warned me not to do it. I told him everything would be okay."

"The robbery went bad, and someone shot your brother."

"He died in my arms," Tony shouted hysterically. "I watched the life flow out of my brother's body right there in front of me, and it was my fault. How many times have I watched him die? When does it end? When can I have peace in my life again?"

"You've had an incredibly bad experience, Tony. You feel responsible for the death of a young man, and the burden of that responsibility is great. Now, do you ask God to ease that burden, or do you move on with a cross that will span any future adversities?"

"How could God ever forgive me?" muttered Tony.

Eddie smiled. "God knows your heart. He knows you're grieving and has already forgiven you. He wants you to move on. He wants you to always remember your brother and the love you have for him, but He also wants you to take this mistake, grow from it to become a better man. With that and God at your side, you can face any gorge, ravine or canyon that life throws at you. You become a better and stronger man ready to redeem your sins by helping some other unfortunate soul in this world. You owe that to God, and to that brother of yours. Don't let him die in vain. Who knows, maybe you wouldn't have saved little Jimmy if you hadn't had your terrible experience. Maybe, Jimmy is the one who discovers a cure for cancer and saves millions. But it all begins with you. Are you going to pick up that cross and save another Jimmy, or are you going to take the easy road?"

Tony paused then fell into Eddie's open arms.

"I love you, Father Rinehart," said Tony.

"I love you too, son."

They remained in that embrace for several moments until Eddie said, "Still want to open that kitchen?"

Tony leaned back and smiled. "More than ever."

"I'll tell you what," said Eddie. "Tomorrow morning, I'll go to the diner by myself. "Every one of those old turds is going to help us with that kitchen."

"How are you going to make that happen?"

"Don't you worry none," said Eddie. "Everyone in there owes me, and I will be there tomorrow morning to collect."

"You have two jobs, and neither one is going to be easy," said Eddie. "Tomorrow, you need to see Cooter. If there's one thing that man can do is to make people do something they don't want to do. If you get him on your side by easing him slowly, he will get you all the food donations you need."

"The man believes I'm an escaped convict. I can't believe he will warm up to me," said Tony.

"Get him started on baseball," said Eddie. "The man loves baseball and probably won't shut up."

"Somehow that doesn't surprise me that a man named Cooter would love baseball," said Tony.

"He claims the Yankees wanted to sign him up when he was a kid, but there aren't too many people in town who believe him."

"What's my second job?" asked Tony.

"You need to go see Belva Bowdry," said Eddie. "She's been a cook all her life, and they don't come any better."

"Do you think she will do it?"

"I don't see why not," said Eddie. "She already loves you for reuniting her with her son."

"I don't know. She's kinda cranky."

"Belva is a woman of few words," said Eddie. "You will be a hit if you get to the point."

Tony slowly rubbed his head. "My head hurts."

"The good news is it will only get worse," said Eddie.

"That's the good news?"

"You haven't done this many times, have you?"

"This is my first."

"Gonna do it again?"

"Not if my head is going to hurt like this."

Eddie grabbed Tony by the arm and got to his feet. "Come on. Let's go to bed."

"I can't think of a better place to be."

CHAPTER TEN

Tony turned the pick-up truck onto a gravel driveway and parked near the front of the house. Belva was sitting on the front steps with a big pot in her lap. She was snapping green beans in half and dropping them into the pot.

"Good morning, Mrs. Bowdry," said Tony as he sat down next to her.

Belva didn't look up. She didn't even miss a beat snapping her beans. "I thought I told you to call me Belva. Even smart ass kids call me that. Why not you?"

"Well, I guess I just thought that…"

"What's on your mind anyhow," she said without looking up. "Ya didn't come out here for nothin'."

"I was told to get right to the point when it came to dealing with you."

"Who told you that?"

"Father Rinehart."

"That doesn't surprise me," she said. "He's right, but in your case I might make an exception."

Tony grabbed a handful of beans and started snapping. "Why is that?"

She stopped and turned to Tony with the slight hint of a smile. "You brought my boy back to me. Besides, I'm a fair judge of character, and I'd say you're a pretty good kid."

"Well, thank you…Belva," said Tony.

She returned to snapping her beans. "So, what did you need from old Belva?"

"I need you to be a cook again."

She stopped and stared straight ahead. "No way in the world," she said.

"Now wait a minute, Belva…"

"My days of cooking are over. The only thing I cook now is something to feed my boy and me."

"I was told that you are the best cook in the county."

"I've had my share of compliments," she said. "But that doesn't change my mind. My cooking days are over."

Tony paused. "Sorry to hear that."

Belva stopped snapping and dropped her pot to the next step. "Alright, what's this all about?"

"Huh?"

"Who do you want me to cook for?"

"I'm going to offer a free meal for anyone who wants one?" said Tony. "We're going to cook and serve it at the church."

"Is that so?" she said. "Where are you going to get the supplies and food?"

"I'm going to get Cooter to collect from all of the businesses in town."

"Good idea," she said. "Who thought of that?"

"Father Rinehart."

"Well, it's going to take more than just you and me to pull this off," she said.

"Father Rinehart is recruiting the breakfast boys down at the diner," said Tony.

She turned to Tony. "You're not serious."

"That's what he said he was going to do," said Tony. "Why?"

"That bunch of misfits couldn't even cook a pop tart, and I know darn well they've never washed a dish in their lives."

"Should I go and stop him?"

Belva huffed. "They'll never do it in the first place. They're all too lazy. I'm surprised they have the energy and ambition to travel up there to that diner every morning. The only incentive is the food."

"So, what do you say…Belva?" Tony asked.

"What do I say about what?"

"Are you going to be my cook? Sorry to say there's no money in it."

Belva picked up her pot and began snapping beans. "What do I get?"

Tony smiled. "A warm, fuzzy feeling?"

Belva paused then began to laugh. "Okay. You got your cook, but you keep those old idiots from the diner away from me. You hear?"

***

It was nearly an hour later that Tony opened the door to the county jail. Cooter was asleep leaning against the wall with his feet on his desk. Tony slammed the door. It startled Cooter was much he jerked and sent him crashing to the floor. He scrambled to his feet, turned his chair upright and sat back down.

"What can I do for you, boy?" he said.

Tony paused.

"Oh, sorry about that boy business," said Cooter. "The thing is, I call everybody boy. It's just a habit with an old turd like me. Now, I know you and your kind don't particularly care for that name, and for that I apologize. Didn't mean anything by it. Just an old habit. That's all. Now what can I do for you?"

"I need to ask you a question," said Tony.

"Fire away," said Cooter. He then put his hand up to his mouth. "Sorry. Poor choice of words. I know you and your kind like to carry guns seeing as how you live in those bad areas of the city. I gotta tell ya that I've often wondered why you people would want to move into such a neighborhood. Don't make sense. There are so many nicer places to live."

Cooter paused as he studied Tony's face. "I swear you're the one in that picture. I don't care what the Reverend said. I'd bet the farm that you're the escaped convict. Now what do you say to that?"

"Well, I think…"

"I hope you noticed that I didn't mention the fact that you and your kind all look alike. Did ya happen to notice that? The county has forced me to take what they call sensitivity training. I have to go to some class over in Marion once a week to learn how to be sensitive when I'm around people. Good Lord, there ain't nobody more sensitive than me in this town or in these whereabouts. And you can take that to the bank. It all started when I pulled that little gal over for speeding. Damn, she was cute. I swear she was cuter than a speckled pup. Anyways, she went and told her uncle that I was hittin' on her, and he just happened to be the county sheriff. The next thing I know I'm taking these dang sensitivity lessons. I guess they've done me some good. Hell, you don't want to know what I might have called you if I hadn't had them. Did you ever have to take sensitivity lessons?"

"I can't say as I have."

"Well, there is one bright spot about the whole thing," said Cooter. "The teacher is a real looker. I'm a fixin' to ask her out. She might be a just a bit out of my league, but you know the old saying, nothing ventured, nothing gained. I figure the worst that could happen is that she would tell me no. I know it's hard to believe, but she won't be the first to turn down ole Cooter. No siree. She would just be another in a long line of females who missed out on a night out with the Cooter. Say now, you came over here to see me about something. Maybe I should dummy up so you can get in a word or two."

Tony stared at Cooter half expecting him to start talking again. "We're starting up a soup kitchen kind of thing at the church," said Tony.

"Well, now, ain't that a great idea," said Cooter. "We got a lot of folks around here who ain't had a job in quite some time."

"We plan to put on a meal every Saturday night, and anybody is welcome."

"Well, ain't that the dandiest thing you ever heard," said Cooter. "Who's doing the cooking?"

"I got Belva Bawdry to cook."

"Whoa. How did you get her to come out of retirement?"

"It wasn't easy, but I managed."

"So, why are you telling all this to ole Cooter? You must need something from him."

"We have a cook, and some men to help us, but we need donations of food and supplies," said Tony. "And Father Rinehart said you're the man who could make that happen."

Cooter leaned back against the wall with a smile on his face. He regarded that as a real compliment coming from Eddie. "He did, did he?"

Tony could see that he had him hook, line, and sinker. All he had to do was reel him in. "He said there wouldn't be a businessman in town who would be safe and that you would squeeze every dime out of this town for a good cause."

Cooter's smile got even bigger. "Well, there was that time that the little Simpson girl broke her leg, and her folks didn't have any insurance. I must have raised over five hundred dollars for them."

"See," said Tony. "Father Rinehart was right. You can perform miracles."

Cooter blushed. "Oh, I wouldn't say that."

"And he's modest too," said Tony.

Cooter leaned forward and pointed his finger at Tony. "You know and I know that you're that escaped convict. Even that darned ole Eddie knows as well, but I ain't gonna do nothing about it. No, sir. In fact, I'm turning my head and looking the other way. I'm doing that because you're a good man, Tony. When you first got here, the townspeople were pretty much up in arms, you being a Negro and all. The only reason I didn't haul you off to jail is that Eddie and I go way back. But that's all changed. Little by little, I've been hearing nice things about you. In fact, there are those who say you've changed their lives. Now I don't know what you did to get yourself thrown in prison, but I really don't care because I believe that down deep, you're a good man. I ain't no religious kind of guy, but I gotta believe you were sent here by the Almighty for a purpose. What that purpose is, I don't know. Maybe it's this kitchen thingy you want to do, but I don't think so. I think the big Guy has something else in mind for you."

"Well, thanks, Cooter," said Tony with a modest smile. "That was very nice of you to say that."

"No problem, my young friend. I guess what I'm saying is you're welcome in this town."

"So, does this mean you will do it?" asked Tony.

Cooter stood and thrust out his hand. "I'll get you enough food to feed an army," he said.

Tony stood and took his hand. "Thank you, sir. You won't regret it. I promise."

Cooter pulled back his hand and sat back down. "Now get out of here. I got work to do."

"Oh, by the way," said Tony. "I hear you were almost signed by the Yankees."

Cooter got the biggest smile on his face. "Why, yes that's right. I was…oh, now I get it. That was Eddie who put you up to that. Now go on and get out of here."

***

Four blocks away, Eddie sipped his coffee and scanned the table of men. He had known most all of them his whole life. In fact, he had gone to school with nearly everyone. Some were rich, some were poor. Some were generous and others were as tight as a clam. But the one thing they all had in common was spare time. Oh, they all claimed to be busy, but there wasn't a one of them who couldn't donate a Saturday evening once in a while for such a charitable event. He knew they would all put up a stink and bitch their heads off. There wasn't any doubt about that. Eddie knew he would have to be strong and demanding and quite possibly threatening to this bunch of misfits.

Eddie saw a lull in the conversation and jumped to his feet. "Listen up, you guys. I have something to tell you."

Everyone at the table froze. They knew that Tony had unsuccessfully tried to recruit them for a job, and they were quite sure this would be Eddie's attempt to do the same.

"The soup kitchen that Tony talked to you about is going to happen," said Eddie scanning the table.

"Well, isn't that nice?" said Otis. "Now, sit down and finish your coffee."

"I don't think you dip wads understand," said Eddie with an even louder voice. "Each and everyone of you will be there every Saturday night helping us pull this thing off."

That statement sent grumbling up and down the table.

"What makes you think you can convince us to help you?" asked Otis.

"Sit down, Eddie," said Cletus Trimble.

"Cletus, my old friend and former classmate," said Eddie. "I was hoping you would spew some of your sage wisdom on us and you did. Do you remember about four years ago when that tree fell on the back of your house? Who was it who spent nearly a month helping you repair the damage?"

Cletus hung his head. "It was you, Eddie."

"Remember what you said when we were all finished? You said something about owing me a favor."

"Well, I was…"

"And you, Earl," said Eddie pointing across the table. "Remember when you lost your job?"

"Yeah, I remember," said Earl.

"Everyone in town knows that the church helped bail you out when you needed help," said Eddie.

"I just thought everybody should know," said Earl.

Eddie pointed a finger at Earl. "What you didn't tell them was that you never paid back what you owed to the church."

Earl stiffened in his chair.

"You owe me big time, Earl," said Eddie.

Eddie swung his pointed finger to the end of the table. "And you down there, Willard, do you happen to remember when the court was going to take your kids away? Who was it that spent weeks putting together a case that would convince them to leave your kids with you? You owe me. You all owe me, and I'm collecting right here and now. I expect to see all of you pitiful creatures at the church next Saturday."

He turned to leave then stopped. "And if I don't see you there, I'm coming to your house to collect what you owe...plus interest."

That Saturday night went off without a hitch. Dear sweet Belva was in heaven cooking for a bunch of people, and everyone of those breakfast morons was there. Belva was doing it for the pure joy of it all while I am certain that the guys were just afraid that Eddie would pay them the visit that he promised.

Now we all know that God does things for a purpose. Sometimes we think we know what purpose He has in mind, and then there are times He fools us. Take for example this idea that Tony had for feeding the hungry. There's no doubt that it served a good purpose and was a Godly thing to do, but it was a stepping stone for Tony to get to the place where God wanted him. I'm not so sure God's plan didn't go as far back as the prison break. They say that God moves in mysterious ways, and God's plan for Tony was no exception. The good news was that His plan was about to unfold and be quite evident, and it all started with Tony's eyes falling on a young girl sitting by her mother and she was completely bald. Tony had never seen anything quite like this. He tried not to stare. There were many who would consider that to be, at the very least, rude, and, yet, he couldn't help himself. There was something about this little girl that seemed to interest him. He couldn't explain it, but, nevertheless, he felt in his heart that he had to meet her and talk with her mother.

He began picking up empty plates and trash working his way down the table where they were sitting. As he got closer, they became aware of his presence and began piling trash in the middle of the table.

"How's the ham?" he asked with his attention on the mother.

"Very good," she said wiping her mouth with a napkin. "It had a different and yet wonderful taste to it."

"You can thank our cook, Belva Bawdry," said Tony. "She's one of the best."

"Do you work here?" she asked.

"Yes, I do."

"I can't tell you how much we appreciate this meal," she said. "We were both so very hungry, and I had no idea where we were going to eat."

"Well, let me tell you how happy I am to hear that we could help. That was the whole idea of putting this together," said Tony. "Let me tell you there were times I didn't think this would happen."

"You sound as if this was your idea."

Tony blushed. "May I sit down?"

"Please do," she said pointing at a chair.

"My name is Tony," he said thrusting his hand in her direction.

"Norma is my name," she said taking his hand and lightly shaking it. "And this is my daughter, Bess."

"Hi, Bess," he said.

"Hi," she said shyly.

"How did you like your dinner?" asked Tony.

"It was very good," said Bess.

"Can I get you something else?"

"No, thanks," said Norma. "There are still others filing in the door, and we wouldn't want to deprive anybody."

"Stick around," said Tony. "After we're sure that nobody else is coming, we're going to pass out everything that's left."

"Oh, that's very nice of you, but we're going back home tomorrow after we conduct some business in the morning."

"Where's home?"

"We have a small place over on the other side of Cambridge."

"You're a long way from home," said Tony. "What brings you all the way over here?"

"There is a man near here who is building a place called LaRue. His name is Mr. Joseph. Do you know him?"

Tony snickered. "Oh, yes. I know him. I hope you're not going to work for him."

"Oh, no. Nothing like that. We just want to sign up to stay there for a weekend."

"Why? What's he building? A hotel?"

"You don't know?" she asked.

"Know what?" asked Tony with a smile still on his face.

"When it's completed, LaRue will be a place, a refuge if you will, for families with children stricken with cancer. They will be able to spend a weekend in a log cabin in the woods and everything is free. Even the food is to be donated by local businesses."

The smile disappeared from Tony's face. His mind raced as he tried to understand. "I didn't know," he uttered with a stunned look.

"I could tell," she said. "I've been told that Mr. Joseph is over half done with the place and is signing up people for future weekends."

Tony eased back into his chair. His gaze turned to Bess who by now was smiling at him.

Then it hit him. As he stared blankly at the little girl, it hit him hard. "Are you telling me that Bess here has…?"

Norma forced a smile. "Yes, Bess has cancer."

Tony seemed to collapse in his chair. "Oh, dear God!"

"She contracted it over a year ago," said Norma. "They gave her six months to live, and everyday she proves them wrong. Don't you, Honey?"

Still smiling, Bess simply nodded her head.

Tony paused. "I don't know what to say."

"Don't worry, Tony," she said. "You don't have to be bashful around us. This last year, we've been through it all, hopes and fears, anger, tears. Ask anything you'd care to."

Tony turned to Norma with a blank look. "I had no idea."

"Actually, I would have thought her bald head would have given her away."

He turned to Bess and then back to Norma. "Is this from the cancer?"

"Not directly," she said. "It is caused by her treatments. Ironic, isn't it? The killer itself leaves no evidence. It's a silent killer, and, yet, the treatment leaves behind distinct tracks."

For several moments, the three of them sat there silently, until Tony finally came back to life. "We're going to do what we have to do so that Bess and you can spend a weekend at LaRue," he said getting to his feet. He shook her hand once again. "I promise you that."

"Well, thank you so much, Tony," she said.

"Before you leave here, let's exchange phone numbers, so that I can keep in touch."

"That would be great," she said. "Thanks again."

"Take care, Bess," he said waving his hand.

Bess simply waved back.

Tony wander aimlessly back to the kitchen and nearly bumped into Eddie. He studied Tony's face for a moment then said, "I've seen that look before. Now what?"

"Tomorrow, I'm off to see Larry Joseph," said Tony with conviction.

Eddie smiled. "Well, good luck with that."

CHAPTER ELEVEN

I scooted back my chair and got to my feet. Bishop Livingston looked exhausted as he eased himself back in his chair. "I'm going down the hall to get a cup of coffee. Care for one?"

The bishop stared blankly at the wall and slowly nodded his head. "Yeah, sure," he muttered. As I walked down the hall to get the coffee, the bishop stood and stretched as if he'd been asleep.

"Hope I'm not boring you with my story," I said handing him his coffee.

"Certainly not," he said. "I've been so engrossed, I didn't realize how stiff I was from sitting so long. It would seem that little girl got to Tony."

"She hit him hard," I said. "You know, God shows His hand sometimes. I'm not real sure if He intends to, but His work was pretty obvious when it came to Tony. Even an atheist would have got religion if he had followed Tony's life."

The bishop sipped his coffee. "You mentioned that Tony is going to visit Mr. Joseph at LaRue. Didn't Tony visit him earlier in the story?"

"If you recall, Tony told Eddie that he was sent there by the bishop to help with the building of LaRue. Of course, that went sour as everyone expected."

"Was Mr. Joseph that difficult to get along with?"

"Larry had a heart as big as all outdoors," I said. "But he was as stubborn a man you'd ever meet."

"I think I would have liked to have known this Mr. Joseph," he said. "It would appear that he was a very interesting man."

"The thing about Larry was if he took a liking to you, he'd do just about anything for you. The problem was he never took a liking to anybody."

The bishop laughed. "I would say your Tony had a very interesting life after he arrived in this small town."

"Actually, I didn't think he would make it," I said. "He grew up on the streets of Detroit. Pretty much everything he ever learned, he learned on his own. Coming to a small town made up almost entirely of white people was a cultural shock not only for him but the townspeople as well. For the most part, they treated him pretty fair. Oh, there were a few exceptions. Fred Townsend slipped and used the n word around him, and Earl Bass referred to Tony as a boy. All-in-all, I was pretty proud of the way everyone behaved."

"You make it sound as if they were school children."

"Sometimes they act like school kids," I said.

The bishop sat back down and set his coffee on a small table beside his chair. "Don't keep me in anymore suspense. What happened when Tony went to see Mr. Joseph?"

I sipped my coffee and sat down across from him. "As you might have guessed, when Tony learned what LaRue was all about, he was committed to helping Larry with such a worthwhile project. Seeing that little girl and knowing that she had cancer broke Tony's heart. Whether he knew it or not, he had already dedicated his life to helping others, and this became his number one priority. After all, what could be more tragic than a child dying of this dreaded disease. Tony was now convinced that God put him in that small town to help Larry Joseph create this miracle called LaRue.

It was early morning when Tony pulled into a small clearing in the woods. He parked next to an unfinished log cabin. On the ground leading to the front door were wood forms outlining what was to become a sidewalk. Tony walked around to the front of the building to find Larry mixing concrete in a wheelbarrow. He stood there for several moments just watching Larry work. Larry quickly glanced at his visitor then returned to his work.

"Good morning, Mr. Joseph," said Tony.

"It's Larry to you. Mr. Joseph sounds like someone from the IRS."

"Yes, sir...Larry."

"What are you doing back here anyhow? I thought I told you I didn't want any help."

"I wasn't going to help you," said Tony. "Right up until I found out what LaRue is all about."

"Why should that change your mind?"

"I met a little girl with cancer the other day," said Tony. "She wants to spend a weekend at LaRue, and I want to see her do it."

Larry tipped the wheelbarrow over and poured the concrete into the wooden frames. "Is that so?"

"I know this is none of my business, but what's your motivation for LaRue? Why are you so dedicated to such a place?"

Larry moved the wheelbarrow out of the way and began to smooth out the concrete. "That's none of your business," he snapped.

"You know I half expected an answer like that from you," said Tony. "Why do you have to be so rude?"

"Why do you have to ask so many dumb questions?"

"Are you going to let me help, or what?"

Just then, a pick up truck pulled in and stopped near a picnic table.

"That's my wife," said Larry. "Go help her get breakfast on the table."

An attractive, middle-aged woman got out of the truck and began unloading bags and boxes from the back of the truck. As Tony approached the truck, the passenger door opened, and a beautiful young black girl got out of the truck. She was a bit bashful and shy and after a quick glance in Tony's direction turned to help unload the truck.

Tony couldn't move. He had never seen such a beautiful girl and certainly never expected to see her in a place like this.

"Hi. My name is Tony," he said taking a box from the back of the truck.

"Ah, you must be that young man who is helping Father Rinehart," she said handing him her packages. "Here, take these over there to that table. My name is Annie. Have you met Jen over here? Of course, you haven't. You wouldn't be staring at her in such a manner. Go on and introduce yourself. She's pretty, isn't she? Oh, if you won't do it, I will. Tony, this is Jen, and Jen, this is Tony."

"Nice to meet you," said Tony.

"Nice to meet you," she said shrinking in a coy manner.

They stared at each other for a few moments until Annie interrupted. "Alright you two. We haven't got time for a marriage ceremony right now. Tony, you set that stuff on the bench, and help Jen set the table."

"Mrs. Joseph…"

"Call me Annie."

Okay…Annie," said Tony. "I was sent here to help your husband, but I get the impression that he doesn't want any help."

Annie began making sandwiches. "That would be my Larry. Love that man to death, but land's sakes he is stubborn."

"Is it me? Is it because I'm black?"

"Oh, good Lord, no," she said. "Wouldn't matter if you were the president of the United States. Who knows why he resists free help. The only reason he allows Jen on the grounds is because she is helping me."

"I was here once before," said Tony.

"You were?" she asked.

"Yes, and he pretty much ran me off."

"Damn, he's starting to get on my nerves," she said dropping what she was doing. "Sorry for the potty word, but he really beats all. I'm going to have a little private chat with him before we eat. You two finish up here."

As Annie stormed off, Tony turned to Jen. "So, tell me," he said. "How long have you lived around here?"

"Actually, I don't live here," she said. "I live in Agosta."

"That's five miles away," said Tony. "Do you have a car?"

"No."

"Then how do you get here?"

"I walk."

"You walk all the way from Agosta to help these people? Are they paying you anything?"

"No."

"Then why do you do it?"

"My mother died of cancer," she said. "I want to do whatever I can for those who have been stricken with that horrible disease." She paused. "Why are you here?"

"Well...I don't know," said Tony searching for an answer. "I guess because of your mother, because of a little girl I met with no hair. Actually, it feels like something I must do."

"You don't have anybody in your family who has cancer?"

"No."

Jen smiled. "That's not only sweet but noble as well. You should be proud of yourself."

Tony blushed and said nothing.

"I don't believe the rumor," she said as she spread a tablecloth across the table.

"What rumor is that?"

"There's a rumor around town that you're an escaped convict," she said with a smile.

Tony laughed and spread his arms out. "Now do I look like an escaped convict?"

"How would I know?" she asked. "I've never seen one before."

"Well, they look like anybody other than me," said Tony with a smile.

"Are you really a priest-in-training?"

"You seem a bit skeptical about me," said Tony. "I thought we were beyond that when you realized I came here to help."

"Well, maybe the idea of your being an escaped convict has made me a bit leery," she said with a somewhat angered voice.

"But I told you that I wasn't."

"Why should I believe you?" she demanded. "I don't know you. I've never seen you before in my life."

"Well, that's no reason to call me an escaped convict."

It was about that time that Larry and Annie walked slowly over to the table. "Tony," said Annie. "Larry has something to tell you."

All eyes turned to Larry.

Larry gave a quick, sarcastic glance at Annie. "You can help me...just don't get in the way."

"See. That wasn't so hard, now was it?" said Annie. "Now let's all sit down and eat."

Everyone took a seat around the table and started eating. The mood was quiet. There was tension in the air.

"So did you two get a chance to get acquainted?" asked Annie.

Tony and Jen exchanged glares.

"Oh, we know all we need to know about each other," said Jen with sarcasm.

Annie glanced at the two kids and realized that they hadn't hit it off. "How's your sandwiches?" she blurted.

"I have a question," said Tony. "Why are we eating sandwiches for breakfast?"

Annie laughed. "Oh, that's right. You're new here. You see, Larry starts work at four in the morning. This is lunchtime for him."

"Oh so, because Larry here can't sleep at nights we eat baloney for breakfast," muttered Tony.

Larry turned and gave Tony a disgruntled look. "I told you this kid was going to be a problem."

Tony dropped his fork and turned to Larry. "Now how can you say something like that? I'll bet I can out work your old butt any time of the day."

Larry said nothing. He simply shook his head.

"Is it because you don't think I'm strong enough?" asked Tony. "Is that it?" He placed his elbow on the table and extended his hand. "Wanna arm wrestle? Come on, Mister Tough Guy. Let's see how strong you really are."

Larry turned to Annie. "I'm going to kill him." He placed his elbow on the table next to Tony's and grabbed his hand. "Say when."

For a few moments, the two men stared into each other's eyes.

"When," said Tony.

The two hands locked together. It was obvious that Tony was struggling while Larry merely grinned at his competition. Then, as if he tired of the whole affair, Larry slammed Tony's arm to the table.

"Okay, Wise Guy," said Tony. "You caught me off guard. Let's do it again."

Larry muttered something and got up from the table. "Thanks for lunch, Annie. I've got to get back to work," he said and walked away.

Tony scrambled to his feet and followed him across the lawn. They stopped at the half-finished cabin. It was nearly seven feet tall with much more to go. There was a pile of old weathered logs at one side of the cabin and an enormous pile of logs nearly a hundred feet away.

"These logs look old," said Tony. "Where did you get them?"

"This was a real cabin built in 1835," said Larry. "I found it in Cambridge, Ohio. I bought it, tore it down log-by-log and brought it here."

Tony pointed at the other pile of logs. "What's that all about?"

"That's going to be a barn," said Larry.

Tony surveyed the area. "We need to finish the house and then build a barn, and you want to open next month? Are you crazy?"

Larry picked up one end of a log and started to drag it across the yard. "There are those who have said that."

"You couldn't possibly expect to get all that done even with my help."

Larry turned to Tony. "You know that's your opinion and guess what? I didn't ask for it."

Tony picked up the other end of the log. "See there you go again with that attitude. Why can't we just work together? We don't necessarily have to like each other. Besides, we're both here for the same thing. We want to see these families enjoy a weekend here to get away from bills, work, and even more importantly get away from cancer."

They hoisted the log and dropped it into place. Larry dropped his hands to his sides and turned to Tony. "Okay," he muttered.

"Okay, what?"

"Okay, let's work together," said Larry. "After all, you won't last more than a couple days."

"What do you mean by that?"

"You're a city kid. You don't know a darn thing about working hard."

"You don't know that," said Tony.

"Are you going to be here tomorrow morning by four?"

"Hadn't planned on it."

"See what I mean."

"That doesn't make me a bad worker."

"Well, what does it make you?"

Tony gave a sarcastic smile. "It makes me a normal person who likes to sleep until daylight."

The two men lifted another log and dropped it in place.

"Tell me, Larry," said Tony. "What inspired you to take on such a project? Did you run across a little girl with no hair?"

Larry stopped and looked Tony in the eyes. "I'll let you work here with me but please don't ever ask me that question again."

Tony stepped back a bit. "Whoa, where did that come from?"

Larry turned to pick up another log, and Tony scrambled for the other end. Tony sensed that this subject was closed.

As brutal as it was, Tony made it through the first day. With his back aching and his head hung low, Tony limped into the parsonage. Wanda was washing the last of the dinner dishes while Eddie drank a cup of coffee at the kitchen table. He dropped into a chair and laid his head on the table.

"Are you alright?" asked Eddie.

"I'm not sure," said Tony. "My back broke some time early this morning, and I haven't been able to feel any other parts of my body."

"Did Larry work you pretty hard?"

"I'm surprised he didn't strap a saddle on me."

"Sorry, my friend, but this was your idea," said Eddie.

"Don't remind me."

"How was Larry when you left him?"

"He was planning to work for another two hours," said Tony. "I don't think he even broke a sweat."

Eddie had been holding back the laughter. He couldn't stand it any longer and let it all out. "Sorry, but it's almost as if city boy meets country boy."

Tony lifted his head from the table. "The worst part is I need to be back there at four in the morning."

"It's good for you," said Eddie then muttered, "If you survive."

"I don't know how he does it," said Tony. "He never tires or even takes a break. If it wasn't for Annie, I doubt he would stop to eat."

"He's a big man with a strong back."

"Don't I know it?"

"Hungry?" asked Wanda.

"I'm too tired to work my jaws," said Tony. "Since I'll have to get up at three to be there by four, I'm off to bed."

"It was nearly 4:30 when Tony pulled into Larry's driveway. He could see that Larry was sitting on a pile of wood. He stopped the truck, crawled out and hobbled across the yard.

"You're a half hour late," said Larry.

"That's the least of my problems," said Tony easing himself on the pile next to Larry.

"What's the matter with you?" Larry asked.

Tony slowly shook his head. "I got sore parts on me I didn't even know I had."

Out of the corner of his eye, Tony could see Larry wince. "What's wrong with you?"

"Nothing. Why?"

"You looked as if you were in pain."

Larry stretched and yawned. "Oh, just having trouble getting started this morning."

Tony jumped down and started doing a stretch exercise. "Give me a second to loosen up," he said. He glanced at Larry to see his face skewed as if he were in severe pain. Tony stopped what he was doing. "Are you okay?"

Larry leaned back and took a deep breath. "Yeah. I told you once before I was okay," he said then jumped off the pile of wood. "Now let's go to work."

It was nearly noon when they finally knocked off for lunch. As usual, Annie was there with hot lunches for both of them. There was hot meatloaf, mashed potatoes and coffee to drink and enough food to leave both of them muttering to themselves why they ate so much.

Larry, by nature, was a quiet man. That day he seemed even less talkative. As Annie cleaned up after the meal, Larry, suddenly, announced that he was going for a walk. Tony and Annie stared at each other in surprise then turned to watch the big man disappear into the woods.

"What was that all about?" asked Tony taking a seat at the table.

"Sometimes he likes to be alone," she said sitting next to Tony.

Tony smiled. "You love him very much, don't you?"

"It shows that much, huh?"

Tony slowly nodded his head.

"He's been my whole life ever since I met him."

Tony stared at the spot where Larry disappeared into the woods. "I couldn't help but notice that Larry seemed to be in some pain."

"Wouldn't surprise me," said Annie. "The doctor told him he shouldn't be working."

"Why is that?" asked Tony.

"He had a hernia operation just last week," she said. "When the doctor told him that he can't be working like this, he told him to put in an extra layer of mesh and a few extra stitches because he had too much work to do. The doctor wasn't too concerned. He figured that the pain from the hernia operation would prevent Larry from working, and you see how that worked out."

Tony stared into the woods. "Good Lord, how does he do it?"

"I've wondered the same thing," she said. "He's a strong man and yet one of the most sensitive men I've ever known. I remember a time when the neighbor kid's baseball rolled down the street and fell into the rain gutter. The kid was devastated, and I could see that it broke Larry's heart. When the kid finally gave up trying to get it out of there and went home, Larry tried his best to retrieve the ball. When he finally realized that it had most likely been carried away by a current of waste water, Larry got into his truck, drove into town and bought that little boy a new baseball. That, essentially, is Larry Joseph. All kids love that man, and why not? He loves all kids. There are those who claim he was the best and most beloved teacher who ever lived in this part of the country. I don't doubt it. There are millions of stories out there about that man. It's amazing to me that such a big man and a strong man at that could be so sensitive and kind to just about everyone he has ever met."

Tony turned in her direction. "Then why does he hate me so much."

"Larry doesn't hate you," she said with a smile. "In fact, he admires and respects you for trying to help him. It's just that right now he has so much on his mind what with the cancer and all."

"Oh, yeah," said Tony. "The kids...the kids with cancer."

Annie paused and slowly turned to Tony. "You don't know, do you?"

"Know what?"

Larry...Larry has cancer."

"Oh, my God," said Tony with a look of shock. "He's going to be alright, isn't he?"

"No, I'm sorry," she said. "At best, he has a few months to live."

Tony covered his face with his hand and turned away. "Oh, dear God," he muttered.

"I thought you knew," she said softly and placed a hand on top of his.

Tony wiped his eyes and took a deep breath. "And here all along I thought his race was the deadline for the first family to spend a weekend."

"The day we learned that Larry had terminal cancer, we ran into a little girl about seven or eight years of age. She was coming into the hospital for treatments as we were leaving. Of course, she had no hair and was moving rather slowly for such a young child. Larry saw her go by. He stopped and watched as she disappeared down a hallway. I could tell his heart was breaking. He tried to disguise the tear that trickled down his cheek, but I knew. I knew what was going on inside that man's heart. As he turned and walked towards the parking lot, it hit him. Oh, yes. It hit him hard. I had seen that look before and knew that we were in for trouble. He told me he wanted to build a place where cancer kids could spend a weekend free of charge. It would be a place where there was no cancer, no bills, no doctors and best of all no pain. I asked him where we were going to get the money. He said that he didn't know. I asked him where he was going to get help to do it. He said that I shouldn't worry about such things, and I asked him why not. He said that God would take care of the details. Well, here we are just weeks away. We sold just about everything we had including our life insurance, but we now own seventy acres, a log cabin and a barn. God took care of the details alright, but He put everything on our tab."

Both Tony and Annie smiled.

"All I want and pray for is that Larry can live long enough to see that first family playing games in the back yard, going for hikes in the woods and enjoying the peace and quiet."

"I don't mean to pry and this is certainly none of my business, but what are you going to do? You sold your life insurance, and you might lose Larry."

"Oh, I'll have to admit. I've thought about my future and the problems I might have to face alone, but you see this is Larry's dream. I think his dream is to leave something behind to tell the world that he was here, that he made a difference. I can't imagine why. There are thousands of adults out there who were students of his, and I know they would say that he made a difference. Everyone needs a dream, and this is Larry's dream. As his wife and lifelong mate, it is my duty to see to it he reaches that dream."

Tony sat there for several moments digesting what had been said. His heart ached for Larry and even more so for those young boys and girls stricken with this monster called cancer.

Then it hit Tony. He turned to Annie who was drying her eyes. "I need you to get Larry out of town for a couple days."

"What?" asked Annie.

"I need you to get Larry away for just two days. I know how to get this LaRue completed so he can stop killing himself."

"Actually, we are going out of town next week," said Annie. "He has an appointment at the cancer clinic in Billings, Montana. We'll be gone for three or four days."

"That's perfect," said Tony rubbing his hands together. "When you return, LaRue will be completely finished."

"How in the world…"

"Never mind," said Tony. "Just have a good time, and I'll take care of everything."

***

It was late afternoon when Tony pulled into Frank Bower's driveway. A tall, burly man with an attitude checked his credentials and when he discovered Tony's name, gave him the royal treatment by escorting him to Frank's office. As soon as they opened the door, Frank got to his feet and leaned over his desk with an open hand.

"Mr. Franko," said Frank. "How nice to see you."

"It's Tony," he said taking Frank's hand.

"Please, have a seat," said Frank pointing to an open chair.

Tony sat down and leaned back in the chair. "How's that grandson of yours?" he asked.

"He's doing great," said Frank. "Thanks to you."

"Well, that's fantastic."

"So, tell me. What can I do for you?"

Tony leaned forward in his chair. "You know I didn't save your grandson's life expecting some kind of reward."

"That goes without saying," said Frank. "But I still want to do something for you."

"Well, it just so happens that I need a favor," said Tony. "And this is a case of one good turn deserves another."

"Just name it."

"You've heard about Larry Joseph and his efforts to build LaRue."

"Actually, Larry and I went to school together," said Frank. "I think his idea of building LaRue is a great one."

"Let me come to the point," said Tony. "Larry is going to be out of town next week, and I want you to finish building LaRue."

Frank settled back in his chair. "What did Larry say about this?"

"I'm not telling him," said Tony. "You know as well as I that he would never approve it."

"Then why are you doing it?"

"Larry is hurting really bad," said Tony. "He just had a hernia operation and should be off for weeks. The work is too high off the ground and should be done by machine. If I wasn't helping him, he'd be somehow doing it by himself. The poor man is dying of cancer and deserves a break. For God's sakes, no man should be going through the hell he's going through during his last few days on earth."

Frank paused for a moment then smiled at Tony. "I'll take care of it, Tony Franko," he said extending his hand. "You will get your wish, and Larry will get his LaRue."

Tony shook Frank's hand. "Thank you, Mr. Bower."

"It's Frank to you."

A week later, Larry and Annie got home from their trip to Montana. Larry got out of the car and scanned the grounds. At first, Annie wasn't quite sure how he was going to take it. He was too proud to accept help, and yet he was tired, much too tired to finish the construction of LaRue.

He turned to Annie with no expression on his face. "Who did this?"

"I think it was Tony," she said with a bit of apprehension in her voice.

It was about that time that Tony pulled up in front of the cabin. He got out of the truck carrying a bag of groceries. Larry began walking at a rapid pace towards him. Annie was nearly running to keep up. As Larry stepped onto the front porch, Tony came out of the building standing on the same porch. He was looking up at the big man when Larry stuck out his hand.

"I want to personally thank you for what you did," said Larry.

Tony took his hand. "My pleasure," he said. "You looked like a man who deserved a break."

"All the way home from Montana, I was wondering how I was ever going to finish the work."

"It was my opinion that it's time for you to relax and enjoy," said Tony.

"How did you do it?"

"Tony laughed. "Now that's not very polite."

"You didn't do it yourself," said Larry with a smile. "I know how you work."

"Well, now you're getting downright rude," said Tony laughing aloud.

"Come on."

"Frank Bower owed me a favor, and I collected."

"Must have been a big favor," said Larry.

"That's not all," said Tony. "Frank is going to stock your pantry as well."

"That's incredible," said Larry.

"So why don't you and your lovely wife go on home and rest up from your trip? You must be tired, and I've got some odds-and-ends to do."

Larry glanced first at Tony then to Annie. "Let's do it," he said with a smile. "Let's go home."

On July 23rd, Larry stood proudly on the porch of a log cabin built with purpose and loving care. As the first family to spend a weekend in that same cabin climbed the steps, Larry welcomed the mother and the father by shaking their hands. As a timid and shy seven year old girl with no hair stepped onto the porch, Larry fell to his knees. He tenderly took one of her hands and gently held it in his. As tears welled in his eyes and spilled down his face, he took the young girl in his arms and held her close. All the doubts and uncertainties he might have had about this project called LaRue were put to rest.

Larry died a year and a half later. God was gracious enough to allow Larry to see 22 families spend a fun-filled, worry-free weekend at a place called LaRue. Every doctor who ever examined Larry said he should have died two years ago. It wasn't only his stubborn determination that kept Larry alive but his love for young people as well. His legacy lives on not only through the thousands of former students but the continuation of LaRue as well. Supported solely by donations, Annie Joseph bravely carries the torch that was handed to her by a big man with a big dream.

CHAPTER TWELVE

I leaned back in my chair and took a deep breath. Bishop Livingston was visibly shaken by the story. He was staring blankly at the wall as if he were still trying to absorb all that I had told him.

"I do have a question for you," said the bishop. "Frank Bower seemed to soften a bit near the end. Did he ever change his attitude towards the Amish?"

"Ah, I'm glad you asked that," I said. "There is a very interesting story connected with that. We had a tornado go through our little town. Fortunately, it only came near the downtown area. It tore a path down through the corn and soybean fields with a vengeance. It did manage to get close enough to Frank Bower's ranch that it greatly damaged his barn. The worst part was it tore nearly the entire roof off of it. What's even worse, Frank was in the barn at the time. He was a very fortunate man in that he owned such an incredibly well built barn keeping him virtually safe from harm. He was hit in the head by a flying piece of the roof and spent over a week in the hospital. There never was any danger of Frank losing his life, but the bump on his head was very serious. In fact, he was unconscious for days. While he was in the hospital, a most remarkable thing happened. The Amish almost immediately loaded supplies and marched over to the Bower ranch. They began working on that damaged barn and, by the time Frank had returned home from the hospital, they had repaired all of the damage and had put on a new roof. When one of Frank's workers told him what had happened, Frank was a changed man. In spite of the disrespectful and oftentimes malicious way he treated the Amish, they disregarded all that and came to his aid. When asked why they had performed such a miracle, they answered that Frank was a neighbor, and it was their duty to help him out."

"Did Frank ever repay their efforts?" asked Livingston.

"As a matter of fact, he did. The first thing he did was eliminate the dams that were holding back water that flowed to the Amish farms."

"How 'bout that young girl that Tony met?" Livingston asked. "They seemed to have gotten off to a bad start."

"They dated a few times, but Tony knew in his heart what he was going to do for the rest of his life, and that had no room for a woman."

Livingston sat straight in his chair. He turned an ear towards Rinehart's room. "I hear a groan," he said.

We rushed into his room to find him not only awake but trying to sit up in bed.

"Eddie," I said. "I knew you were too stubborn to leave us."

Eddie looked at me, and, of course, expected to find me there but was a bit bewildered to find Bishop Livingston leaning over his bed. "Bishop Livingston, what a surprise."

"How are you feeling, Father Rinehart?" he asked.

"I'm not real sure," said Eddie. "What are you doing here?"

"Well, I was...I guess you might say..."

"Well, I'll be," said Eddie. "You folks didn't expect me to pull through." He turned to me. "Tony, I'm surprised at you. As long as we've been friends and you would think I would leave without saying goodbye."

Livingston turned to me. "You're Tony?"

I smiled rather sheepishly as if I had been caught doing something wrong. "Yes, I'm Tony."

"I thought your name was O'Brian," said Livingston.

"I made him change his name," said Eddie sitting up in his bed. "Never did like that Franko business. Made him sound like some godfather or something evil like that. So when he was ordained, I made him change his name."

"You wanted him to be an O'Brian?" asked Livingston.

"He couldn't change it to a Jefferson or a Brown," said Eddie. No, he had to go and be a smartass and change his name to O'Brian. I think I hate that worse than Franko."

Livingston turned back to me. "Why didn't you tell me?"

"Well, it started off being a quick story," I said. "I was hoping to give you a little background on this man without any involvement, but it all got kinda carried away. Besides, I got so I enjoyed referring to myself in the third person."

"Well, you certainly fooled me," said Livingston with a smile.

The smile on Eddie's face disappeared and he leaned forward just a bit. "Bishop Livingston, I wonder if you might leave Tony and me alone for a moment. I have something private to discuss with him."

Livingston stood straight. "Why certainly," he said and walked out of the room.

I watched as he disappeared and turned back to Eddie. "Now what's so important?"

The smile I was expecting on Eddie's face did not reappear. I now knew this was serious business.

"Tony, we've been friends for a good many years. I've loved and trusted you more than anybody I've ever known in my life. There is something I want you to do for me when I'm gone."

"Oh, you're not going anywhere," I said trying to ease the seriousness of the moment.

"Yes, I am, Tony," he said looking me in the eyes. "I know that God was kind enough to give me this last brief moment with you, my best friend, because of this unfinished business."

I could hear the cold seriousness in his voice and could read it in his eyes. "What is it, Eddie?" I asked.

"I want you to help Annie Joseph. If this had happened years ago, I would have devoted nearly all of my time to help her raise the money that she needs."

"I heard that she was doing okay," I said with a reassuring voice. "Half the people in that town are helping her to raise money."

"You don't understand," said Eddie. "she needs in the neighborhood of $80,000 each year to keep that place operating. She is an incredible woman, but she could use the help."

"Good Lord, I had no idea she needed that much money."

"Insurance alone is alone is an incredible amount not to mention the food, electric bill and so forth."

"Okay, Eddie, you have my word," I said. "I will do what I can to help her."

Eddie settled back into his bed still with a solemn look on his face. "In a few hours, I hopefully will get to meet God, and if I do I just want to ask him one question. Why would you allow young children to get cancer?"

I wiped the tears from my eyes and made an effort to smile. "You old turd," I said. "You'll outlive me anyhow."

He sat up once again. "Tony, trust me. I was spared only long enough to make these provisions. There is no tomorrow for me, only the assurance that my writings are in good hands. I'm sorry for handing this burden to you, but I have no other choice. You are my lifelong friend, and I am passing the torch onto you."

I smiled at the old man as he settled back down in his bed once again. "You don't put much pressure on a friend, do you?"

"Go on and get out of here," he said dismissing me with a wave of his hand. He then rolled over as if to say that he was going to sleep.

Father Edward Rinehart died later on that night. A nurse was there beside him at the time. When asked what his last words were, she recalled that he muttered something, and the only part she could understand was something like, "And Lord." I smiled when I heard her say that because I never forgot his favorite hymn and knew she was wrong. I knew what his last words were because I knew the name of his favorite hymn was called, "Here I am, Lord."

THE END

ABOUT THE AUTHOR

In 1996 with a lifelong dream of being a writer, Scott Fields started writing short stories. Within the two years, he had four stories published. Since then, his first novel, *All Those Years Ago*, was published, and in the fall of 2004, his second novel, *A Summer Harvest,* was released. His third novel, *The Road Back Home*, was published in the fall of 2007 by Charles River Press, and his fourth novel, *Last Days of Summer*, was released by Whiskey Creek Press. *Summer Heat*, his fifth novel, was published in May 2012 by Outer Banks Publishing Group. To date, Scott has published 13 novels.

Scott and his wife, Deb, live in Mansfield, Ohio.

The Mansfield Killings - It was the worse two-week killing spree in Ohio's history.

On the night of July 21, 1948, Robert Daniels and John West entered John and Nolena Niebel's house with loaded guns.

They forced the family including the Niebel's 21-year-old daughter, Phyllis, into their car and drove them to a cornfield just off Fleming Falls Road in Mansfield.

The two men instructed the Niebels to remove all of their clothing, and then Robert Daniels shot each of them in the head.

The brutal murders caught national attention in the media, but the killing spree didn't stop there. Three more innocent people would lose their lives at the hands of Daniels and West in the coming week.

Scott Fields tirelessly researched the killings, the capture and trial of Daniels and even interviewed a surviving member of the Niebel family to weave this tragic story into a gripping, must-read novel bringing the reader back to those dark days in the summer of 1948.

What led to these brutal killings, and why was the Niebel family singled-out and savagely murdered remains a mystery to this day.

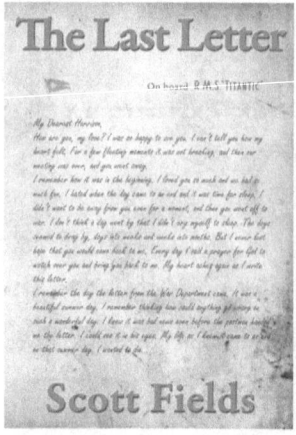

The Last Letter - From her watery grave at the bottom of the Atlantic Ocean, the Titanic, even today, guards secrets of the past.

A woman, reportedly died that fateful night when the Titanic sunk, and yet she lived until the year 1995. Why did she feign her death all those years ago, and now after she's gone, why is she trying to send a message to the living?

This is the untold story about the Titanic that has been kept secret for over one hundred years.

The Last Letter is novel about two people drawn together by the hand of a woman that neither had ever met. Together, they set out to fulfill the unconsummated relationship of two people who met and fell in love over one hundred years before.

Breakfast at the Diner - It has been two years since the death of his wife, and Frank Watson still struggles with the loss. Every morning, he meets with his friends at the local diner to talk and to exchange gossip, but inevitably must return to his farm that remains undisturbed since his wife's death.

Then, Pepper Ledley breezed into his life. She was the new waitress in town nearly half his age and offered Frank something he had never considered…a new beginning.

However, it somehow didn't seem right to Frank. How could he have these feelings when he still loved Ida?

The Killing Road - Dale Marlowe drifted from town to town, taking odd jobs when he ran out of money until he met Rachel Armstrong and fell in love for the first time in his life.

Shortly after they were married, Dale seemed to settle into a steady job and married life until his obsession raised its ugly head.

He went back to heavy drinking and soon Rachel and Dale were auguring almost non-stop.

Dale had had enough and went back to his drifting, but this time instead of taking odd jobs, he took people's lives.

What ensued was a multi-state killing spree and not a single police force could track him down until he raped and killed the sister of a retired policeman and his brother.

Erv Meyers and his brother, Kramer, became as obsessed as the killer to find Marlowe and bring him to justice in one of the most elusive manhunts in criminal history.

The story is based on actual events.

A Killing in a Small Town

- Harlan Steelman owned most of the town of Bear Creek and found his way in and out of every backroom, barroom, and bedroom.

When his rival from high school, John Watson, returns to Bear Creek with his wife and son to start anew, Harlan vows to ruin John's life and take Kara, his wife, away from him.

When Harlan is found murdered, John Watson is the likely suspect and is taken into custody.

What happens next is the trial of the century for the little town of Bear Creek, but it takes a horrible twist at the end.

Summer Heat - A hot summer, a sultry town flirt whose husband was away and an opportunity she had never faced. What followed was a series of sordid events involving murder, deceit, betrayal and the conviction of an innocent man in this erotic novel.

All of Scott's books are available on Amazon in print and as ebooks as well as in fine bookstores everywhere.